TALES FROM A LONG ROOM

Peter Tinniswood was born in Liverpool. He is the author of six highly praised novels including *A Touch of Daniel*, *The Stirk of Stirk* and *Mog*. His BBC television series 'I Didn't Know You Cared', which featured the unforgettable Brandon family, has become a comedy classic and will shortly be the basis of the National Theatre's first musical. Peter Tinniswood is currently working on a new novel.

He has not yet been asked to open the batting for Lancashire but he once spoke to Winston Place.

D0794713

Also in Arrow
by Peter Tinniswood

More Tales From a Long Room

TALES
FROM A
LONG
ROOM

Peter
Tinniswood

ARROW BOOKS

For my dad
who took me to my first
cricket match.
And for my mum
who bought the Tizer
and packed the sandwiches.
And to their grandchildren:
Stephen, Vicky, David and
Beth with my love.

Arrow Books Limited
17–21 Conway Street, London W1P 6JD
An imprint of the Hutchinson Publishing Group
London Melbourne Sydney Auckland
Johannesburg and agencies
throughout the world
First published 1981
Reprinted 1981 (three times), 1982 and 1983 (twice)
© Peter Tinniswood 1981
Illustrations © John Lawrence 1981

This book is sold subject to the condition that it shall
not, by way of trade or otherwise, be lent, resold,
hired out or otherwise circulated without the pub-
lisher's prior consent in any form of binding or cover
other than that in which it is published and without
a similar condition including this condition being
imposed on the subsequent purchaser.

Set in Linoterm Sabon
by Book Economy Services, Cuckfield, Sussex
Reproduced, printed and bound in Great Britain by
Hazell Watson & Viney Limited,
Member of the BPCC Group,
Aylesbury, Bucks
ISBN 0 09 926620 8

Contents

Introduction

I was born in winter.

I love the summer.

My friend the Brigadier was born in Arlott St Johns.

He loves fine claret, Vimto, quail in season, barrage balloons, blotting paper, E.W. Swanson and his sister Gloria.

He recounted these tales to me during the course of a long and convivial summer spent in his favourite corner of a long room 'somewhere in England'.

Peter Tinniswood

1
Root's Boot

During the course of a long and arduous career in the service of King and country I have had the honour in the name of freedom and natural justice to slaughter and maim men (and women) of countless creeds and races.

Fuzzy wuzzies, Boers, Chinamen, Zulus, Pathans, Huns, Berbers, Turks, Japs, Gypos, Dagos, Wops and the odd Frog or two – all of them, no doubt, decent chaps 'in their own way'.

Who is to say, for example, that the Fuzzy Wuzzies don't have their equivalent of our own dear John Inman and the delicious Delia Smith, mother of the two Essex cricketing cousins, Ray and Peter?

I have no doubt that the Dagos have their counterpart

of our Anne Ziegler and Webster Booth, and I am perfectly certain that the Wops, just like us, have lady wives with hairy legs, loud voices and too many relations.

Indeed it is my firm opinion that all the victims of this carnage and slaughter were just like you and I – apart from their disgusting table manners and their revolting appearance.

Poor chaps, they had only two failings – they were foreigners and they were on the wrong side.

Now as I approach the twilight of my life I look back with pleasure and with pride on those campaigns which have brought me so much comfort and fulfilment – crushing the Boers at Aboukir Bay, biffing the living daylights out of the Turk at the Battle of Rorke's Drift, massacring the Aussies at The Oval in 1938.

But of all these battles one remains vividly in my mind to this very day – the Battle of Root's Boot.

The incidents pertaining to this conflict occurred in 1914 during the MCC's first and only tour to the Belgian Congo.

Who on earth had the crass stupidity to give the Congo to the Belgians in the first place is quite beyond me.

I am bound to say that I consider the Belgians to be the most revolting shower of people ever to tread God's earth.

Eaters of horse flesh, they let us down in two world wars. They're hopeless at golf. They drive on the wrong side of the road, and they're forever yodelling about their blasted fiords and their loathsome fretwork eggtimers.

Is it any wonder they made such a confounded mess of running the Congo?

When we went there in 1914, there was not one decent wicket the length and breadth of the country, and the facilities for nets were totally inadequate.

And, if that weren't enough, during our matches there were at least two outbreaks of cannibalism among spectators, which I found totally unacceptable, and which I am convinced were responsible for the loss of our most promising young leg spinner, M.M. Rudman-Stott.

He was sent out to field at deep third man in the match against an Arab Slavers' Country Eleven, and all we found of him after the tea interval was the peak of his Harlequins cap and half an indelible pencil.

But of these setbacks we were blissfully unaware as in high good spirits we set off from Liverpool in April 1914 aboard the steamship, SS *Duleepsinjhi*.

The party was skippered by the Rev. Thurston Salthouse-Bryden, a former chaplain to Madame Tussauds and a forceful if erratic opening bat who distinguished himself in 1927 playing for the Convocation of Canterbury by scoring a century before matins in the match against a Coptic Martyrs Eleven.

I had the honour to be vice captain and OC ablutions, and among the notable players in our midst were the Staffordshire opening bowler, Thunderton-Cartwright, who was later to become rugby league correspondent for *The Lancet*, and the number three bat and occasional seamer, Ashton, F., who was later responsible for the choreography of the Royal Ballet's highly acclaimed production of *Wisden's Almanack*, 1929, featuring

Alicia Markova as Ernest Tyldesley.

Of all the players in the party, though, the one who made the profoundest impression on all who met him (and some who didn't) was the all-rounder, Arthur Root, a distant cousin of the Derbyshire, Worcestershire and England player, Fred Root, of the same name.

Root was what we in the 'summer game' call 'a natural'.

During the voyage he kept us constantly entertained with his reading in Derbyshire dialect of the works of Colette, and his rendition on spoons and stirrup pumps of the later tone poems of Frederick Delius.

Root had charm, wit, erudition and the largest pair of feet it has ever been my privilege to encounter.

Indeed on the outward voyage they were directly responsible for saving the life of a Goanese steward who fell overboard seven nautical miles sou' sou' east of Ushant.

The poor wretch was applying linseed oil to the Rev. Salthouse-Bryden's self-righting lectern when a freak giant wave washed him overboard.

With the lifebelts being in use for a rumbustious game of deck quoits, Root with great presence of mind threw the only object available to him into the sea – to wit, his right boot.

The dusky Indian steward clambered into the pedicular container and was instantly hauled aboard by the boot laces.

Little did we realize then how vital that boot was to be to our safety and well-being many many months later.

We disembarked without incident at Matadi and set

off forthwith for the interior.

What a noble sight our native bearers made as they trudged along the primitive jungle trails carrying on their woolly heads the essential paraphernalia of our expedition – sight screens, portable scorebox and heavy roller.

The capital city, Leopoldville, was reached in three weeks.

How strange it was to our English eyes – no tram conductors, no Bedlington terriers, no Ordnance Survey bench marks.

Our only consolation came when Root discovered the local branch of Gunn and Moore's where we bought leopard-skin cricket bags, scorebooks bound in genuine okapi hide, and the Rev. Salthouse-Bryden purchased an object warranted as a Bantu baptismal love token, but which to my untutored eyes looked more like H. M. Stanley's left testicle.

We won each of our four matches in Leopoldville by an innings and 'a substantial margin', the Belgians ground fielding, as we had anticipated, being of a typically abysmal level.

A nation of congenital butterfingers, the Belgians.

We then set out for what was to be the most difficult and dangerous opposition of our entire tour – three unofficial Test matches against the Pygmies.

We left Leopoldville on a sultry August morning and did not reach our destination until late November 1914.

During the long and onerous trek we had the misfortune to lose three members of our party:

Evans-Pritchard, E. E.: stung by scorpion.

Leakey, L. S. B.: trampled by buffalo.

Attenborough, D.: retired hurt.

It was a nuisance to lose two wicket-keepers and a 'more than adequate' middle order batsman in that fashion, but nonetheless our party was in good spirits, when we arrived at Potto Potto to be greeted by officials of the Pygmy Board of Cricket Control.

The chairman, a gnarled, wizened little creature, who, incidentally, bore a marked resemblance to the distinguished light comedy actor and chanteuse, Mr John Inman, made us most welcome, offering us victuals and a choice of his most beautiful wives.

'Just like playing for Derby against Notts at Worksop,' said Root, and one and all joined in his hearty and innocent laughter.

On the advice of the Rev. Salthouse-Bryden we declined the feminine offerings but accepted the victuals which were served in the great adobe, thatched pavilion by elderly matrons of the tribe.

It was during the subsequent revelries that the first hitch in the proceedings occurred.

By prior arrangement we were to provide the balls to be used in the match, and, as a matter of courtesy, our baggage master, Swanton, presented a box of same to be examined by the Pygmy officials.

Imagine our horror when the minute, dark-skinned fraternity passed the balls from hand to hand, sniffed them, shook them and, with expressions of sublime delight, ate them.

Worse was to follow when the severely truncated tinted gents offered us the balls they wished to use – row upon row of small spherical objects, gnarled, matted, wrinkled and pitted.

For a moment we gazed at them in stunned silence.

Then the Rev. Salthouse-Bryden exclaimed:

'Saints preserve us – they are shrunken heads.'

What could have been the very severest of fraught situations was saved by our ever-genial giant, Root.

Picking up one of the heads in his massive fist, he examined it briefly and then said:

'Don't worry, skipper. We'll use this 'un. It should be just right for seaming after lunch.'

The day of the first unofficial test dawned bright and clear.

The Pygmies won the toss and elected to bat.

The two Pygmy openers made their way to the wicket to the accompaniment of the howling of monkeys and the screeching of gaudily feathered parakeets, and as I watched them take the crease from my vantage point at deep extra cover, it was for all the world like looking through the wrong end of a pair of binoculars at a dusky wee George Wood and an extremely sunburned Mr Harry Pilling.

Our opening bowler, Thunderton-Cartwright, came bounding to the wicket to deliver the first ball of this historic match.

It whistled from his hand at ferocious pace.

But all to no avail.

On the puddingy and unresponsive pitch the ball thudded mutely into the turf and rose no more than six inches from the ground.

'Bouncer,' yelled the Pygmy opener.

It was a cry taken up in unison by the masses of minuscule spectators packed in dense masses in what was, I believe, their equivalent of the Warner Stand.

An ugly incident seemed certain to ensue.

But at that moment, totally unexpected, came the crackle of small arms fire, and across the distant river burst a column of native Askaris.

As the Askaris waded across the river, firing indiscriminately from the hip, the Pygmies fled as if by magic.

As bullets whistled past our ears we flung ourselves to the ground, only to hear the following words which plunged an icy dagger to the depths of our hearts.

'On your feet, Englische Schweinhunds!'

We looked up to see three white men, dressed in khaki drill, with shaven heads and leering duelling scars upon their cheeks.

'Huns,' we cried in unison.

Indeed they were.

Why hadn't MCC informed us that war had been declared?

Why hadn't the Test and County Cricket Board notified us that marauding parties of German colonial troops were rampaging through the territory?

Why was there no news in *The Cricketer* of the conflagration that was to rewrite the map of Europe and suspend for four years all Test matches between England and Australia?

Such thoughts flashed through my mind as we were bound by the straps of our cricket pads to the portable scoreboard, and the Askaris lined themselves in front of us in firing squad formation.

It was then, as death stared us in the face, that we were addressed by our skipper, the Rev. Salthouse-Bryden.

'Oh, Lord,' he said. 'Thou hast in Thy wisdom decreed that our innings shall be closed.

'It is pleasing to Thine eye that in that great score-book in the sky it shall be written of our party, "Death stopped play".

'So, Lord, give us the strength to face the long walk back to the celestial pavilion like men and members of the MCC, or whichever is more appropriate.'

It was at that moment that I noticed that Root was improperly dressed for the occasion.

His right boot was missing.

Before I could speak he motioned with his eyes towards the distant river.

An amazing sight met my eyes.

Floating silently in the current was a large right cricket boot.

And in it, paddling silently, was a war party of our erstwhile Pygmy opponents.

The Huns and Askaris, totally unaware of the approaching sporting footwear, paused to gloat over their triumph.

It was to be their undoing, for in an instant the boot touched the river bank, the Pygmies sprang out through the lace holes and, screaming like dervishes, unloosed their poisoned arrows against them.

It was all over in seconds.

The Askaris and their vile Teutonic masters lay dead at our feet.

The match was resumed the following morning.

We had the good fortune to win, when Root took the last three Pygmy wickets with the last three balls of the match.

Years later he was to maintain that this was only possible owing to the slight inconsistency in the second new ball, which caused him to produce prodigious variations in swing and bounce.

And with a smile and a gentle nod of his genial head he would say:

'I reckon it were the duelling scar in the seam what done it.'

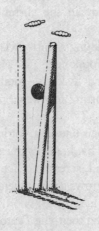

2
Our Own Dear Queen

It is a fact not generally known that in her youth Queen Victoria had the makings of a cricketer of considerable stature.

Indeed it is the opinion of many historians of the 'summer game' that but for the cares of state and the burdens of excessive childbearing, she could well have reached Test match standard.

Contemporary records reveal that the young Victoria was endowed with an excess of the cricketing virtues – the athletic grace of a Frank Woolley, the snow-white teeth of a Learie Constantine, the combative pugnacity of a Freddie Trueman, the dark, hairy legs of a W. G. Grace.

There are many experts who firmly believe that after her death Queen Victoria achieved reincarnation in the form of Mr George Duckworth of Lancashire and England.

While the resemblance, facially and vocally, cannot be denied, I myself tend to the view that, if reincarnation did take place, it came in the shape of Mr B. D. 'Bomber' Wells of Gloucestershire and Nottinghamshire.

His broad beam and the slow waddle to the wicket before delivery of the ball always seemed to me to have a regal quality that was not to be explained by Altham coaching manual, but bore all the hallmarks of a person well used to the state opening of colonial parliaments and the rigours of nineteenth-century confinement and pregnancy.

Dear 'Bomber' Wells!

How different the history of our beloved country and, indeed the wide world beyond, might have been had he acceded to the throne in 1837 – though I am bound to say I have slight doubts about his ability to cope with the demands of Prince Albert of Saxe-Coburg-Gotha.

This odious German princeling has in my view cast a dark, malign shadow over this country, which to this very day has still to be lifted.

How else to explain the benighted summer of 1980 with its long and dreary succession of rain-affected county cricket matches, its dripping sight screens, its sodden squares and its elevation to the prime minister-ship of a woman with the manners of an ink monitor and the charm of a power-mad swimming baths atten-dant?

How else indeed?

I believe passionately that most of the great calamities of this century can legitimately be placed at the feet of this nauseous German princeling – the loss of Empire, the decline of pride and patriotism, the enfeebling of manly courage and vigour, the demise of the leg spinner, the retirement from the *Daily Telegraph* of Mr E. W. Swanton, father and grandfather respectively of that celebrated Hollywood film star, Miss Gloria Swanton.

Do I exaggerate? Do I overstate my case?

I think not.

Consider this.

Had this country been ruled in its pomp and in its prime by a monarch who had played Test match cricket, opened the innings for her country at Headingley, been struck in the ribs by Spofforth at The Oval, smashed in the teeth by Gregory at Old Trafford, bitten on the buttocks by the groundsman's ferrets at Trent Bridge, is it conceivable that Britain should be in its present desperate plight with women newsreaders on the moving television screens and threatened centre-page pin-ups of Brian Johnston in *Wisden's Almanack*?

Nothing will dissuade me from the opinion that had Queen Victoria been allowed to develop her cricketing ability to its fullest potential, this dear country of ours would still be 'mistress of the seas', 'mother of the free' and holders *in perpetuum* of the Corbillon Cup.

And what relevance has Prince Albert to this?

The answer is simple.

He it was who forbad his wife, his youthful, fresh and innocent bride, from wielding the willow, donning the pads and weaving her subtle spells with the crimson rambler.

Let us consider the facts calmly and objectively. The historical canon relates that Queen Victoria first met her putative consort at Windsor on 10 October 1839.

This is not, in fact, the case.

In an appendix omitted in somewhat mysterious circumstances from Heygarth's *Scores and Biographies* there is a reference to a cricket match held in June 1838 at Crabbe Park, in which Queen Victoria, playing for William Blunt's Eleven, took seven wickets for seven runs and struck three successive sixes off the redoubtable F. W. Lillywhite.

She scored an undefeated 87 in 23 minutes, the ferocity of her hitting being only matched many years later by Mr G. L. Jessop, and the fluency of her stroke play having no equal until the arrival of 'the silken-shirted Hindu', Mr K. S. Ranjitsinjhi, whose descendants incidently now run a most agreeable Tandoori chicken restaurant on the outskirts of Keating New Town.

Unknown to our so-called academic historians, with their limp bow ties and discoloured waistcoats, Prince Albert was in the close vicinity of the cricket ground engaged in business of a quite different nature.

He was on an unofficial visit to this country, examining and evaluating the latest developments in animal husbandry and land management.

It was while he was in a neighbouring field inspecting a novel and amusing device for the instant decapitation of poachers that he was struck a violent blow behind the left temple by a ball smitten out of the ground over deep square leg by Queen Victoria.

He was knocked unconscious.

On regaining his senses he inquired as to the nature of the blow which had caused an irregular egg-shaped protruberance to appear on his close-cropped, bullet-shaped cranial extremity.

'Lord save us, sir,' said the farmer. 'Tis the Queen what done it. It must be her batting. The stumper is standing up at the wicket.'

There and then Albert resolved to marry the young Victoria, daughter of Edward, Duke of Kent, niece of Leopold, first King of the Belgians, and devoted drinking companion of Mr Fuller Pilch.

Why did he make this decision?

I believe that at the very moment the leather-bound sphere struck his temple there was released in him all those primeval stirrings of violence, bestiality and brutality inherent in the soul of every Hun who ever lived.

A woman who could inflict pain!

A woman who could knock unconscious a man in the prime of his life!

She must be his.

Nothing less could satisfy the loathsome yearnings of his black Teutonic heart.

The marriage took place on 10 February 1840.

The *Encyclopaedia Britannica* states that the Queen was 'dressed entirely in articles of British manufacture'.

This was indeed the case.

For under her dress of purest Macclesfield silk she wore Gunn and Moore cricket pads, Daymart thermal string vest and Gray-Nicolls abdominal protector made out of stout Sheffield steel and covered with the tartan of the Gordon Highlanders.

Later that evening in the bridal chamber as the young Queen commenced to disrobe, the Prince was enchanted by what, to his untutored eye, was the novelty of this garb.

The sensuous slap of cricket pads against chaste and pristine flesh as his new bride practised her off drive, the tumble of silken hair over smooth young shoulders as she removed her I Zingari cricket cap, the faint, exotic whiff of Sloane's liniment as she wheeled over her arm in that distinctive 'square on' delivery style aroused in him strange, exciting and not unwelcome feelings of desire in the nether regions of his popping crease.

It was with a happy and pumping heart that he retired to his nuptial bed.

Imagine his chagrin when his young bride insisted on taking a net before joining him in the conjugal container.

It is my belief that the humiliations he suffered that honeymoon night contributed more than anything else to his subsequent gravity of mien, his humourless, grinding, rigid code of morals and his ceaseless and finally successful efforts to stop the young queen's cricketing activities.

Picture the scene that honeymoon night.

The young bride crouches at the wicket.

The young groom, clad in night shirt and velvet smoking hat, trots stiffly to the wicket.

And in his first three deliveries bowls two long hops and a daisy cutter.

Could any man suffer greater humiliation on his wedding night?

Could anything be more designed to strengthen his will to turn his ebullient, feckless and vivacious young spouse into the authoritarian, dour and austere woman, whose devotion to the duties of state and childbearing was awesome in its comprehensiveness?

Nine children!

No wonder she had such trouble with her run up.

But let us consider the reasons for this prodigality of progeny in greater detail.

Was it really the full and riotous flowering of the maternal instinct?

Was it, in fact, something more than the altruistic desire to provide spouses for a whole legion of European kings, archdukes and landgraves, whose descendants to this very day are to be seen bathing topless without togs on the beaches of southern France and providing their endorsements to the boards of loathsome companies engaged in the manufacture of microwave ovens and digital toenail clippers?

I think so.

Let the dark facts speak for themselves.

It is historically indisputable that after her marriage Queen Victoria refused steadfastly to abandon her cricketing proclivities.

Despite all her husband's despotic discipline she was frequently to be seen opening the batting incognito for Quidnuncs and the Free Foresters, carousing in the back parlour of The Bat and Ball at Hambledon and pulling the heavy roller with 'the best of them' at the White Hart Hotel in Bromley.

In vain did Prince Albert remonstrate with her.

In vain did he appeal to her sense of responsibility

and duty.

There was only one thing for him to do.

Involve her in a constant succession of pregnancies.

This he did, secure in the knowledge that no man in the history of the 'summer game' had ever played Test cricket successfully after the third month of pregnancy.

His plan was propitious.

By the time of his death Queen Victoria's cricketing activities had entirely ceased and her beloved Gray-Nicolls abdominal protector lay rusting in an obscure and dark corner of the royal mews and her prized Geoffrey Boycott autograph cricket bat was relegated to ceremonial duties at the Tower of London.

When I now think of our dear Queen's long reign, I do not think of a monarch who saw vast tracts of the atlas shaded pink and the creation of an Empire on which the sun never set.

No, I think of and mourn the passing of a lady who could, had her immense talents and inclinations been allowed to run their natural course, have been the finest all-round cricketer of her generation and, when age took its inevitable toll, could have developed into an umpire of the most outstanding calibre.

Who is to say, in fact, that she has not already achieved that eminence in the personage of Mr Bill Alley?

—3—

The Ditherers

Of all the happy memories I cherish from my long association with the 'summer game', some of the most precious spring from carefree days spent in the company of The Ditherers.

History does not recount when this touring cricket club was established.

It is well known, however, that from its earliest days it has always had the closest and most cordial military, colonial and thespian associations.

Its presence has been recorded in accounts of the Peninsular War, when a group of British officers, taking a net at the lines of Torres Vedres, was surprised by a squadron of Walloon irregular cavalry and massacred for the loss of all ten wickets.

Contemporary Chinese silk prints of the period seem to suggest that The Ditherers played a number of matches during the Boxer Rebellion.

Indeed one of the characters depicted, dressed in surgical sandals, wincyette cummerbund and Free Foresters' thermal underwear, bears a marked resemblance to the distinguished theatrical producer, Sir Peter Hall, brother of the equally distinguished West Indian Test cricketer, Wes.

It was a few years later during a tour to the Trucial States that The Ditherers' deputy stumper was captured by Arab slavers and was not seen again until the early 1930s when an MCC raiding party discovered him in the court of a minor Saudi princeling, where he occupied the position of chief scorer to the royal harem.

Despite his protestations he was bound and gagged and smuggled back to England in the false bottom of a Slazenger cricket bag.

For many years until his death he was to be seen, a lonely and bedraggled figure, skulking in shop doorways in the vicinity of the headquarters of the Ladies' Netball Association of Great Britain.

It was around this time that I began my long and happy association with The Ditherers.

I was staying with relations at the picturesque Lancashire village of Cardus-in-Ribblesdale when The Ditherers arrived to play the local cricket team.

Unfortunately, a series of accidents, involving among others, an infected cricket bat and a rumbustious evening with members of the Rochdale Hornets Ladies rugby league team, had much depleted their numbers.

Much to my delight I was invited by their skipper, the young Glamorgan 'leg tweaker', Ivor Novello, to play for them, and, going in last man down, had the pleasure of both scoring the winning run and taking our side's score into double figures.

Thus began five decades of 'cricket wandering', which has taken me to some of the most enchanting and magical spots on the face of the earth and given me a treasure chest full of fond recollections of fellow tourists, both military and theatrical.

How well I remember that blissful tour of Albania, when Elsie and Doris Waters notched an unbeaten opening partnership of 234.

How well I recall that tour of Greece, when Noel Coward played havoc with Eleven Gentlemen of Athens.

He also performed quite adequately on the cricket field, too.

Still etched on my memory is our tour of Southern India, when for five solid weeks the whole party was laid low with the most violent attack of the Nawab of Pataudis. (On reflection I think that 'solid' is not the most appropriate of words to describe those five weeks of agony.)

That apart, nothing can erase from my mind's eye the picture of the future saviour of civilization as we know it, Lord Mountbatman, saving our match against Bangkok Brotheliers in a last wicket partnership with Mrs Simpson, future Duchess of Windsor and mother of the Australian Test skipper, Bobby.

If, however, I were asked to name my most precious souvenir of my membership of The Ditherers, I would be compelled to say that it was the friendship I formed with our baggage master, Wisbeach.

Ernest Henry Bismark Wisbeach was what we in the 'summer game' call 'a character'.

His physical appearance suggested someone who had spent a great deal of his youth teaching greyhounds how to cheat at racing, and his manner suggested one whose adolescence had been spent in the company of Mafia hit men, Corsican bandits and Yorkshire opening bowlers.

Wisbeach was a man of 'many parts'.

In addition to his talents for farmyard impersonations and forgery, he was also a considerable poet 'in his own right'.

He it was who penned those memorable lines, which seemed to encapsulate all that was most noble and manly from the carnage and horror of the First World War:

> I seen a Hun.
> He had a gun.
> I run.

He was also a noted purveyor of pithy and pungent graffiti.

One of the finest examples of his work was created during The Ditherers' tour of Vienna in the mid-1930s.

It is to be seen in the urinals of the Staatsoper and runs as follows:

'Mozart is a wanker.'

Underneath, written in typical German script, someone has added the legend:

'And so is Emmott Robinson.'

Despite Wisbeach's reputation for unwarranted beligerence, foul table manners and personal uncleanliness, I myself always found him to be a most loyal, entertaining and diverting travelling companion.

In fact, I think I can say without immodesty that he took a shine to me immediately on our first meeting.

This friendship was cemented during The Ditherers' visit to Paris in 1935, when by an unfortunate chain of circumstances, which to this day are too painful to recall, I found myself incarcerated in prison wrapped in a horse blanket and having in my possession a black velvet garter, a bent bulldog clip and the left lapel of Mr Leslie Sarony's smoking jacket.

Wisbeach it was who extricated me from this predicament. I never asked how.

He did not encourage discussion on this matter, although he seemed well satisfied with the annuity of several hundred pounds he insisted I assign to him immediately after my release from prison.

Many people have asked me how it was that Wisbeach, considering his total incompetence as a baggage master, managed to hold down his job with The Ditherers for so many years.

I am bound to confess that he was indeed deplorably deficient in the execution of his duties.

Without any difficulty whatsoever I can recall disasters involving the loss of our portable heavy roller and horse on the Simplon-Orient Express in 1932, the loss of nineteen sets of cricket bats and a crate of Cooper's Oxford marmalade during the tour of Peru and the loss of Oscar Rabin and Miss Shirley Abicair during the tour of the Andaman Islands.

No, I am as baffled about Wisbeach's continuing

employment as all the other members of The Ditherers, most of whom, coincidently, I discovered many years later, appeared to be paying annuities of one sort or another to our erstwhile baggage master.

Most curious.

But nowhere near as curious as Wisbeach's behaviour and subsequent disappearance during The Ditherers' tour to America in 1939.

As always on these occasions Wisbeach insisted on making all the travel arrangements himself.

Our Hon. Sec. had in the past complained about this, but on being taken into a corner by Wisbeach and whispered to in the most conspiratorial and threatening of manner had always withdrawn his objections with a rapidity which to this very day I still find extraordinary in the extreme.

Still, despite our forebodings about the travel arrangements, we were all in high good spirits as we arrived at Liverpool in the late summer of 1939 looking forward with the keenest anticipation to a crossing of the Atlantic by Cunarder.

Imagine our horror when we discovered that the vessel in which we were to cross 'the briney' was not a noble ocean liner, but a foul-smelling, rust-streaked tramp steamer, the SS *Bernard Manning*.

Our accommodation, too, I am bound to say, fell far short of our expectations.

I never really fully mastered the art of climbing into my hammock in cricket pads and protector, and during the storms which increased in ferocity as the voyage progressed, life in our communal lower decks cabin grew hazardous in the extreme as the cricket balls, which had broken loose from their packing case, whirred about our heads like howitzer shells.

We were puzzled, too, on our first night at sea to find Wisbeach dining at the captain's table while we were consigned to an exceptionally unstable trestle table in the darkest recesses of the dining saloon.

However, as the great E. R. Dexter once wrote most perceptively, 'Every cloud has a silver lining'. The ship began to pitch and toss and yaw in the most frightful manner and we were all given invaluable slip fielding practice as we endeavoured to catch the ship's biscuits, which flew from our enamel plates in every direction.

That night as we huddled in our cabin, blessing the tarpaulin covers we had borrowed from the Oval and under which we sheltered, we considered our plight.

What to do?

Mutiny was mooted, but when reflecting upon the plight of numerous Yorkshire cricket professionals who had taken similar action, this notion was swiftly abandoned.

Our specialist cover point suggested mass suicide.

This had its attractions to us all, but when our skipper pointed out that such action might adversely affect our membership of MCC, this notion, too, was abandoned.

No, there was nothing to do but 'grin and bear it'.

For the next six days the conditions of our existence bordered on the intolerable.

Three sets of nets were washed overboard before we had even time to tack our matting wicket to the deck.

Our portable score-box was smashed to smithereens where it stood on the port side davits.

Our first choice opening bats, Dame Flora Robson

and Dame Anna Neagle, had in extremes of terror taken refuge in the crow's nest and, despite the entreaties of our utility off-spinner, Mr Victor Sylvester (leader Mr Oscar Grasso) refused to come down.

Our misery was complete.

On the evening of the seventh day, however, our fortunes changed in the most drastic manner.

We had only been locked in our cabin for ten minutes when, quite without warning, the wind abated and the seas assumed a still, deathless calm.

We looked at each other in astonishment.

Our amazement was instantly increased when the ship's engines stopped.

Then high above us we heard footsteps on the upper decks and the ship's siren hooted softly three times.

In an instant our stumper, Miss Ethel Revnell, hoisted Mr Nosmo King upon her broad shoulders and instructed him to look out of the porthole and report on what he saw.

His subsequent monologue caused us to gasp in wonderment.

Its essence was as follows:

In the sylphlike beams of the moon he saw a boat being lowered from the side of our ship.

It was rowed by four sturdy seamen.

And, standing upright in its stern sheets was – yes, it was Wisbeach.

But whither was that boat bound?

The answer was swift to present itself.

A creaming of waters.

A snarling of muffled engines.

And then out of the salty depths appeared, with water

streaming from its flanks, a submarine.

No.

A U-boat.

(At this juncture Lord Baden-Powell collapsed in a dead swoon, inflicting terminal damage on his woggle.)

Our ship's boat crew drew alongside the German warship and, wonder of wonders, Wisbeach stepped aboard.

And the last Mr Nosmo King, or indeed any of us, saw of our baggage master was his distinctive figure standing upright in the U-boat's conning tower, his right arm held stiffly aloft and pointing at the moon.

Our tour of America was not a success.

I often wonder if our playing record might have been different had we not spent seventeen days in open boats after the German U-boat torpedoed our vessel.

I often wonder, too, what became of Wisbeach.

There are those who maintained that he was appointed baggage master to the German Afrika Korps in the Western Desert, pointing to the fact that in papers left after his death there is proof that Rommel was paying an annuity of £230 per annum to Wisbeach.

I myself take a more charitable view.

I believe that he was, in fact, a secret agent sent by MCC to assassinate Adolf Hitler, but with typical incompetence he failed in his mission, and the Führer survives to this very day in the form of Mr Kerry Packer.

4
'Backstop'

It is my proud boast to say that I have read and indeed known many of the finest scribes and writers associated with our great 'summer game'.

How the names trip off the tongue: Neville Cardew, R. C. Robertson-Hare, Bruce Woodcock of *The Times*, who achieved greater fame early in his career as a pugilist of distinction, and E. W. Swanson, father and brother respectively of that uniquely glamorous star of the moving kinematograph, Miss Gloria Arlott.

But none of these celebrated writers in my opinion compares in style, in wit, in vision and in depth of knowledge with 'Backstop'.

What pleasure beyond compare he gave to countless

generations of 'old sweats' as we served King and country in one of the farthest and most unprepossessing outposts of the British Empire.

I have no hesitation in saying that without 'Backstop' the *Rangoon Weekly Clarion and Trumpeter* would have been just another 'rag'.

Antony had his Cleopatra, Callard had his Bowser, Goethe had his Daisy, Eddie Waring had his Gillow – and so did the *Clarion and Trumpeter* have its 'Backstop'.

How eagerly we awaited delivery of that journal in those scented tropic evenings, serenaded by the languid whirr of the punkah, the muted duskings of monkey chatter and the steady, comforting rasp of our lady wives shaving their armpits.

The routine was ever the same.

Friday evening. The week's labours over. Pink gin. Quinine tablets at hand to ward off the inevitable post-curry attack of the dreaded Nawab of Pataudis.

And on to the verandah would pad our faithful Indian jock-strap wallah, Umrigar, his innocent liquid brown eyes beaming with pleasure as grovelling on hands and knees he would present us clenched in his snow-white teeth the latest copy of our beloved *Clarion and Trumpeter*.

I would wrench the rolled-up newspaper from his oriental dental impedimenta and in an ecstacy of delight belabour him about the head and shoulders in a manner which his descendants were to find all too familiar in an encounter with Mr F. S. Trueman many years later in 1952.

Then, dismissing the wretch with an affectionate cuff

round the popping crease, I would seat myself on my Frindall patent portable umpire's commode and settle myself down to an evening's reading.

Ah, the bliss.

Joy unbounded withstanding even the presence of the lady wife staring at me unblinkingly with her piggy little eyes as she knitted another of her interminable muslin trench comforters for her supercilious pet macaw, Dexter.

A quick flick through the pages of the newspaper and there on the back page he would be revealed in all his glory – 'Backstop', a haven of old England in a storm of unspeakable alien loathsomeness.

To me and to many like me, 'Backstop' was the epitome of home in all its nostalgic glory. One had only to read the briefest of his highly distinctive prose to be transported instantly to the damp depths of a London 'pea souper' or the sullen plod of shire horses through cloying Cheshire loam.

I am reminded of those far-off days now as I sit in my study.

The gas fire stutters, the home-bound rooks loiter across a lowering sky, the stuffed carcases of Dexter gazes down on me icily from his perch on top of the television set, and I rustle through my old, fading and yellowing copies of the *Rangoon Weekly Clarion and Trumpeter*.

What memories it brings back to me as my eyes wander over the front page and the close-printed lists of small ads.

'For sale – one Nepalese ballroom dancer.'

'Serious gentleman with pointed teeth seeks mature

lady with similar interests.'

'Tall jockey seeks position with very large horse.'

'Home bible readings and colonic irrigation. Reply in strictest confidence to the Rev. G. A. R. Lock.'

I turn over the front page and the following evocative headline springs out to soothe and comfort my tired old eyes:

'By tandem and canoe to the upper reaches of the Irrawaddy.

'An account of "An Adventure" by the Misses Compton and Edrich.'

Dear Miss Compton.

How chaste, how pious, how refined.

How tragic she should end her days in a fatal accident with a jar of Brylcream.

Onwards, ever onwards, I flick through the pages.

'Recent Arrivals at Rangoon on the steamship, *Duleepsinjhi*.

'Surgeon General K. R. Cranston to relieve Mr Pollard as Principal Dental Consultant to Indigenous Shans.

'Col. and Mrs Washbrook to take up appointment with the Inspectorate of Irrigation and Sightscreens, Mandalay.

'The Hon. W. Place en route to Rawtenstall.'

The pages rustle.

My eyes croon to blurred photographs of slim young ladies in flowing white dresses and khaki shin pads, of bandits strung from wayside gibbets, of the haggard faces of dissident Yorkshire professionals banished to the jungles during the mercifully distant savage regime of Ghengis Sellars.

A salty tear trickles from my eye and falls upon page 19 and : 'Simple Recipes for Simple Servants. Number 863. Boiled cricket ball with linseed gravy.'

And now for the last page.

With what anticipation my trembling hands turn over the newspaper.

There.

There it is.

The headline.

'Gentlemen of Burma versus Mr Arthur Gilligan's Eleven of the MCC.'

Ah, memories.

Sweet memories.

But wait!

What is this beneath the headline?

'Owing to unfortunate indisposition, the report of this match has not been compiled by 'Backstop'. At extremely short notice his place has been taken by Rear Admiral Sir Henry Blofeld. We apologise for the resultant hyperbole and litotes.'

Good God.

I remember.

I remember it well.

Let me compose myself and search through the dusty lofts of memory to recall an incident which even now as I dribble whisky down my lap and spill gentleman's relish over the dozing cat brings pain and darkness to my brow.

Let us begin at the beginning.

Let us try to picture the scene at the turn of the century as the young 'Backstop' disembarks from the steamship *Nayudu* at Rangoon.

What does he carry in that battered Gladstone bag and the tin trunk with the rusted flanks?

Beribboned letters from a broken-hearted lover perchance?

A fond mother's portrait in a silver frame?

A treasured fragment of 'Monkey' Hornby's underpants?

Who can tell?

What fears and forebodings pump to the core of that sensitive soul as he sets off into the interior to take up employ as assistant left luggage supervisor with the Grand Central fully authorized and Harmonious Railway?

Who indeed can guess.

'Backstop' has left us no record of those early days in the wild Manipur Hills.

We can only imagine lonely evenings spent teaching Nagas the rudiments of swing and swerve, bleak, monsoon-bound Sundays instructing Kachins in the arts of scorebook compiling, fever-ridden nights of frustration as he endeavoured to impress upon sullen Chins the intricate subtleties of umpires' signals.

We have some evidence of his success in these matters.

In his memoirs of the Burma campaign relating how single-handedly and with one great bound he defeated the hordes of Nippon, the late and much-lamented Lord Mountbatman recalls how once towards the end of hostilities against the Japanese his aide-de-camp received a flesh wound in the right thigh from a stray oriental bullet.

As the aide-de-camp fell to the ground his Chin guide turned to His Lordship with a smile and with a fluent movement that would not have disgraced the great umpire, 'Cheerful' Charlie Chester, lifted his right leg, extended it sideways, tapped it violently with his right hand and held his left arm aloft.

'Damnit,' said Lord Mountbatman. 'The fellow's signalling a leg bye. Yet another example of the great and multifarious benefits I single-handedly and with one great bound have granted to the civilized world as I and a few privileged friends know it.'

How I wish 'Backstop' had been present to disabuse the noble Lord.

But, no, let us not deal with conjecture.

Let us confine ourselves to facts and assert that when 'Backstop' reappeared from his lonely sojourn in the Manipur Hills it was with the rank of Chief Inspector Buffers and Ticket Punchers.

He had with him a native wife, sixteen children of various hue, a deaf Bedlington terrier and a rusting tin leg, on which was stencilled in faded letters the legend 'Not Wanted On Voyage'.

He also had 'a problem'.

There are those who maintain that it was his wife who drove him to drink and to journalism.

As the whole history of newspapers is liberally lit-tered with similar cases, I do not feel qualified to oppose this opinion.

Certainly his wife made a far from attractive impres-sion with her brown, wizened skin, her treble chins, her strident voice, and the hectoring manner with which she addressed her husband – this again is an experience which many journalists of my acquaintance will not find unfamiliar.

If indeed his wife was responsible for 'Backstop's' problem, we can only lament his recourse to 'the demon'.

On the other hand we can only be posthumously grateful to that lady for her influence in introducing her spouse to the world of ink and quill.

For over ten years 'Backstop' graced the pages of the *Rangoon Weekly Clarion and Trumpeter* with his reports of cricketing campaigns.

The prose was ever immaculate, the style unique and the wit and polish unexampled.

There are those churlish spirits who point out that in some of his reports there were faint undertones of undesirable racial bias.

Poppycock.

Who but a prude and pedant of the basest sort could take exception to the following extract, which shows 'Backstop' in all his literary glory?

'Next to the wicket waddled the unmistakeably loathsome figure of the opponents' Burmese skipper.

'The slanted Mongoloid eyes, the greasy, olive skin, the typically untrustworthy shift of the shoulders, the plump, perspiring contours of over-indulgence and indolence proved no match for the noble and upright wiles of the prince of the lobsters, Simpson-Hayward.

'With a sneer to his lips and a contemptuous flick of the wrist the man from the rich and rolling shires of Worcester released the crimson rambler, which, describing a parabola of the most lissom of proportions, came to earth with a lustrous whisper on the smooth breast of green and with a sigh and a slough rose like a fond lover's mast seeking the fig-pink haven of his young bride's bower of pleasure and spat from a perfect full length to wreck the castle of the foul-smelling obsequious Oriental.'

Only a man who had written such resonant prose could have died happily on the morning of the match, Gentlemen of Burma versus Mr Arthur Gilligan's Eleven of the MCC.

Let us not dwell or linger on the circumstances of his untimely demise.

I myself can affirm that three hours before his 'call to glory' he left the premises of the Royal Burma Mounted Tricycle Club in the highest of good spirits.

The groundsman of the Rangoon Ramblers Cricket Club was to maintain forever that there was a smile on 'Backstop's' face as the heavy roller behind which he had taken a token nap in refuge from the heat of the blistering sun lumbered over his prostrate body.

All that was to be heard as the roller proceeded in its inexorable way was the faint sound of tinkling glass.

There are cynics who assert that this was the sound of splintering gin bottles.

I myself believe fervently, passionately, that it was the sound of the glass breaking on the autographed picture of Mr O.S. Nock, which he had carried constantly on his person since his early days with the railway in the Manipur Hills.

Only one thing marred his death.

At the subsequent post mortem when the pathologist opened up his tin leg, it was found to contain battered copies of *Wisden's Almanacks*, 1902-13.

Fortunately 'Backstop's' reputation remained unsullied.

He was indeed fortunate to have friends 'in high places' who were able to suppress the information that it was 'Backstop' himself who had, during his years in the wilderness, masterminded the operation which had come so perilously close to destroying the whole fabric of the British occupation of Burma.

I refer, of course, to the smuggling of *Wisden's Almanacks* to the impressionable and innocent subject peoples of the darkest interior.

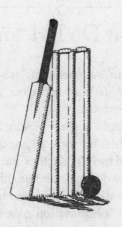

5
What Do I Mean By?

The history of our 'summer game' has been constantly distinguished by its long and close association with 'gentlemen of the cloth'.

How many bucolic country parsons have strapped on their pads, hitched up their hassocks, adjusted their fanons, blancoed their baldachins and strode out on to the cricket field to do battle for thir village team?

How many rural deacons and suffragen bishops have officiated at the solemnization of marriages and the dedication of new lifeboats while secretly wearing under their robes their Free Forester's underpants?

The first-class game, too, has been graced by the appearance of clerics, both humble and distinguished.

A glance at Wisden will reveal that His Holiness, George Pope, gave noble service to the county of Derbyshire for many, many years.

More recently that portly and amiable cricketer, David Shepherd, on his retirement from Gloucestershire county cricket club was appointed Bishop of Liverpool.

And, in my opinion, not before time.

My thoughts have strayed in this direction after recently attending a service at the parish church of St Wilfred, the blessed Rhodes.

The padre there is an old friend of mine.

His name is the Rev. A. K. Mole-Drably, and it is my custom every year to attend the service designated in the Book of Common Prayer as 'The Third Sunday after the Lords Test'.

The church itself is splendid, built in the 'early Headingley' style with its exquisite reredos made from the remains of the sight-screens at Bramall Lane and its magnificent stained-glass windows depicting scenes in the life of Emmott Robinson.

Mole-Drably, a cricket fanatic all his life, took up the living of St Wilfred, the blessed Rhodes, after serving several years as chaplain-general to Sealink.

It was while conducting a service on *The Maid of Orleans* that he achieved episcopal immortality as the only man ever to be seasick while giving holy communion to Mr Wilfred Wooller.

Fortunately for him, Wooller decided not to excommunicate him, a typical act of Christian charity by this near-saintly man, whose name is revered the length and breadth of his native Wales and indeed is the object of cult worship by some of the more primitive peoples of the upper Swansea valley.

It was Mole-Drably's abiding interest in our 'summer game' that was ultimately responsible for his taking over the incumbency of St Wilfred, the blessed Rhodes.

The incident occurred during the annual international cricker *eisteddfod* at Colwyn Bay, when Mole-Drably was acting as umpire in the match Church in Wales Select versus Wynford Vaughan-Thomas.

A chance meeting during the luncheon adjournment with the archbishop of Canterbury, who at that time was Mr E. W. Swanton, later to achieve even greater ecclesiastical eminence as chief cricket writer for the *Daily Telegraph*, was instrumental in Mole-Drably's transference from his maritime ministrations to the quieter backwaters of sacerdotal suburbia.

His Blessed and Overwhelming Reverence E. W. Swanton was leaving the main pavilion where he had been viewing an exibition of Mr Tony Lewis's letters of application to join the National Union of Journalists and listening to a recital of early Carmarthenshire *cynghanedd* with Mr Len Muncer (harp), Mr Gilbert Parkhouse (Velindre bagpipes), Mr Don Shepherd (spoons), and Mr Tony Cordle (mezzo-soprano).

He had lunched well.

The Dee salmon poached in goats' milk and Preseli fennel had been outstanding.

The wines had made sweet and languid music on his palate. He had particularly revelled in a vintage Château Solanky and the arrogant, full-bodied elegance of the Niersteiner Guter Majid Khan.

He was in a benign mood.

At that very moment he had at his disposal two livings, both of which were sinecures in their different manners.

One was the rectorship of St Wilfred, the blessed Rhodes.

The other was editor-in-chief of the *Sunday Telegraph*.

In the full flood of his post-prandial beneficence, he decided that he would offer these livings to the first person he saw on leaving the pavilion.

Thankfully, he did not notice Miss Dorothy Squires slinking out of the Gareth Edwards portable temperance tea rooms.

Instead his gaze fell upon the minute figure of Mole-Drably scurrying to the changing room to don his umpire's garb.

'You!' he bellowed in the manner with which he customarily addressed recalcitrant junior sub-editors and insubordinate captains of England.

Mole-Drably froze in his tracks.

Was it God who had spoken to him?

Had the creator of Heaven and Earth and E.R.Dexter and all the goodnesses thereof chosen to address him in that icy wilderness on the North Wales coast?

Once more he heard those ringing, celestial tones:

'You! Shortarse!'

Scarcely daring to breathe, he turned.

He saw an impressive figure with a leonine mane of snow-white hair and an imperious jut to the jaw.

Yes, it *was* God.

And he was wearing MCC suspenders.

He flung himself on his knees.

And there and then he was granted the benefice of St Wilfred, the Blessed Rhodes.

With what joy he scurried home and flung away the impedimenta of his office as chaplain-general to Sealink – the self-righting dog collar, the inflatable font with snorkel attachment and the bell-bottom cassock.

With what ecstacy he strode down the gravelled driveway of the vicarage of St Wilfred, the Blessed Rhodes, with its rambling roses, its *Leylandi Wilsonia* and its *Erica Sutcliffia*.

And there for the past ten years he has ministered to his flocks with gentleness and humility.

With what tender nostalgia he recounts the highlights of that past decade – his part in the ordination into the BBC of the Rev. F. S. Trueman, his influence on the conversion of Saint Raymond D'Illingworth from his 'Leicester heresy' and his sympathetic intervention during the distressing circumstances surrounding the defrocking of Canon Close.

To my mind, however, it is his sermons which have most distinguished his ministry, and it is with great pride that I reprint the sermon he gave during my most recent visit to his church.

'The text of my sermon today is taken from the following:

"And, behold, Ron Saggers did tour England with the 1948 Australians and, lo, not a single Test did he play in."

'Isn't there a lesson there for all of us?

'The selfless devotion to duty; the debasement of self-interest to the greater good of the team.

'Life is like a cricket tour, isn't it?

'Some of us reach the eminence of an Ernie Toshak.

'Some of us achieve the moderate success of a Doug Ring.

'But for most of us life is a condition of the perpetual Ron Saggers, constant toilers in obscurity, loyal lieutenants to 'the top brass', humble participants in an endless match against Minor Counties on a bleak September afternoon in Jesmond.

'I never met Ron Saggers myself.

'If, however, my Lord and Maker, the creator of E. R. Dexter, Heaven and Earth in that order, were to grant me such joy, I should grasp him by the hand, shake it firmly and say in the manner to which he and his compatriots are accustomed:

'"Good on you, sport. Give my regards to the sheila and let's crack a tube of the old Swans."

'What do I mean by 'a tube of the old Swans'?

'I mean, don't I, that rounded metal object which contains a particularly powerful and nauseous beverage drunk in enormous quantities by our Antipodean cousins and used extensively throughout our great Commonwealth of nations for the dispersal of mosquitoes and the scouring of lavatory pans.

'Life is like a tube of Swans, isn't it?

'For most of us it is a powerful brew, which, if taken in excessive quantities, induces premature baldness and the growth of unwanted hair on the palms of our hands.

'But need we take life in excessive quantities?

'Is there no reason why we should not take it in moderation?

'Let us take a lesson from the cricket field.

'It is the fast bowler, isn't it, who takes all the glory and all the honour.

'But it is the slow bowler, weaving his subtle spells, who ultimately is still playing with distinction and enjoyment long after the fast bowler has "hung up his boots".

'Is it not significant that it was a slow bowler, Mr Eric Hollies, who accounted for the wicket of the great Sir Donald Bradman, in the last Test match he ever played in this country?

'And is there not an example there for all of us?

'If we want to get the most out of life, let us flex our spinning fingers constantly, let us practise diligently in the nets of godliness and always bowl to a good length on the pitch of holiness and never, never play with dirty flannels or dispute the umpire's decision.

'What do I mean by "Umpire's decision"?

'I mean, don't I, those few seconds after the bowler has appealed against the batsman, and we await in a limbo of apprehension as to whether the white-coated gent with the sweaters strung round his waist will raise a forefinger denoting that the batsman is out or turn on his heel shaking his head and muttering:

'"Piss off, you barmy chuff."

'I am reminded here of that great and saintly Lancashire cricketer, Mr Winston Place, who on retiring from the first-class game took up umpiring.

'He resigned from his position, however, because such was his goodness and his benevolence, he could not bear to give people out.

'God is rather like Winston Place, although I suspect

he does not have ginger hair and is not so accomplished a late cutter.

'He doesn't like giving us "out".

'And, of course, if we play a straight bat in the game of life, always move our body into the line of the ball and never flash outside the off stump, there is no reason why God should ever give us "out" until the time comes at the end of the day when the heavenly scorer nods in his drowsy hut and the celestial barmaid places the seraphic tea towels over the ethereal beer pumps, and He declares our "innings closed".

'Let us, therefore, resolve to put on the cricket togs of life with hope and with joy and with love.

'With radiance and gladsomeness in our hearts let us buckle on our pads, shake the dandruff out of our caps, wipe the egg stains off our sweaters and adjust our abdominal protectors.

'What do I mean by "abdominal protectors"?

'I mean, don't I, that device made in former times of metal and canvas and now these days manufactured from reinforced plastic, which men strap over their most private parts to protect them from life's shooters, yorkers and fast full tosses.

'Dear friends, let the love of God be your abdominal protector.

'Let His mercy and His unbounding wisdom be your thigh pad and your lightweight helmet.

'Let His compassion and His clemency for the basest of sinner be your Gunn and Moore jock strap.

'Dear friends, if you want the best out of life, always shop at God's.

'Thank you.

'Next week my text will be:

'"And, lo, Gordon Garlick did smite mighty sixes for Lancashire and then of a sudden was he transferred to Northamptonshire".'

I find that oddly comforting, don't you?

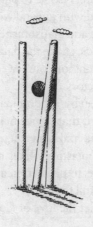

6
The Lady Wife

The lady wife, like most members of her sex (which is female), has an inordinate number of birthdays.

As she grows older these undoubtedly increase in frequency.

Indeed I am of the opinion that she is now celebrating as many as one per annum.

This year, I suppose, she will have a birthday on the Saturday of the Lords Test.

She usually does.

And as always when she informs me of the impending approach of this frightful event, I shall look at her, and I shall think to myself – why?

Why, why, why?

Why on earth did I ever marry her?

Certainly there was a physical attraction. That I cannot deny.

I remember to this day the surge of emotion that coursed through my veins when I first caught sight of her.

The rose garden at dear old Castle Arlott slumbering with honey-laden bees.

The gentle summer breeze lisping through the timid tracery of the delicate Frindall tree.

The Benaud bush aflame in scarlet bloom. The phlox Lakeriensis flowering hazily lazily benignly blue.

And into my view she glided; a tall, slim, sylphlike figure in purest white.

My heart missed a beat.

The sap rose in my loins.

Dear God, she was the spitting image of Herbert Sutcliffe.

It was love at first sight.

Call it the impetuosity of youth if you will, but remember I had been out of the country for many years, serving my King and country in some of the remotest and most primitive outposts of his Empire.

I had not seen a first-class county cricketer for seven years.

I was desperate.

I was bewitched.

I was overwhelmed.

We married that autumn in the exquisite little Saxon church at Witney Scrotum, and as we walked down the aisle arm in arm embarking upon a career of conjugal concomitance I felt for all the world as Percy Holmes must have felt walking out to open the innings for Yorkshire at five past six on a grey, chill September evening at Trent Bridge with Harold Larwood glowering and snarling in the gloom at the Radcliffe Road end.

Our marriage, I am bound to say, has not been all gloom and misery. There have been moments of radiant happiness and unrestrained joy, when it seems that the earth has moved and the heavenly choirs have burst into anthems of passion, and in the soft afterglow I have turned to my wife and said:

'Right, it's your go now. But remember — you mustn't move your legs.'

She always was a duffer at french cricket.

There have been moments, too, when the chores of nuptial incumbency have been enlightened by occasions of solemn levity.

In this context I recall with particular pleasure an afternoon at Cheltenham.

My wife as she approached her prime grew to look more and more like that great Gloucestershire all-rounder, T. W. Goddard.

It was a source of much pride and satisfaction to me, none more so than on that sun-dappled post-prandial session at the Cheltenham Festival, when we were sitting with friends idly nibbling chilled Zubes and supping our mulled Château Dipper.

Our peace and serenity was rudely disturbed when the Gloucestershire skipper, Mr B. O. Allen, strode up to us angrily, pointed an accusatory finger at the lady wife and said in a most hectoring manner:

'Goddard, what in the name of blitheration are you doing there sitting dressed in women's togs? Get yourself off to the dressing room this instant.'

This the lady wife did.

And at the end of the day she had the satisfaction of returning home having taken seven Leicestershire wickets at a cost of a mere seventeen runs.

But moments such as these have been rare indeed in our marriage.

How many nights have I lain awake in bed with soft owls hooting and whiskers of rain snarling at the window pane, and I have raised myself on one arm and looked down at the slumbering form of the lady wife and I have thought to myself:

'My God, I wish you were someone else.'

Admit it, dear friends.

I am not alone in these thoughts.

How many of you while engaged in the most intimate activity in which man and wife can be involved have closed your eyes and thought to yourself at the moment of delivery – by jingo, I wish you were the Nawab of Pataudi.

How many of you have not craved for the warm, passionate propinquity of a Fred Rumsey or the soft, whispered blandishments of a David Bairstow?

Certainly with me it is the 'physical' side of things which have proved most irksome in my marriage.

I am convinced, for example, that it was those bi-monthly Friday night sessions with the light out which were the ultimate cause of a serious weakness in my spinning finger and an inability to achieve a consistent full length.

Nothing will dissuade me from the view that had I not been married to the lady wife, I should have opened the innings for England, captained the Gentlemen against the Players and in the fullness of time achieved the greatest honour any cricketer can attain to – being granted an audience of Mr E. R. Dexter.

Friends tell me that circumstances might have been different had the lady wife and I had issue.

Who can say?

Was Joe Hardstaff, senior, a happier man for having produced Joe Hardstaff, junior?

What gave Mr and Mrs Gibbs more satisfaction – producing one of the finest off-spinners the world has ever known or inventing toothpaste?

Would it have been a consolation to Mr Neville Chamberlain in the darkest days after Munich to know that one day his son, 'Tosh', would play outside left for Fulham?

I think not.

I am reminded of a dear and precious friend of mine, who produced a family of truly extravagant proportions.

I met him in the Long Room at Lords shortly after the birth of yet another of his progeny.

His mien was downcast. His face was bleak.

'Well?' I said. 'What is it this time?'

He looked at me silently for a moment.

And then he muttered savagely:

'Another bloody leg spinner.'

I am bound to confess in fairness, however, that in certain matters of a domestic nature the lady wife has been of help to me.

It was her handiwork with needle and thread which on many occasions has saved me from the distress of having to take a well-loved jock strap to the vet to be put down.

Her dexterity on the fretwork machine saved me from the considerable expense of replacing a sight-screen, groundsman's hut and portable ablutions facility destroyed under circumstances which even now I find too painful to recall.

No, weighing the pros and cons of our marriage in the balance, it is evident to me that but for the frequency of her birthdays, the lady wife might have become a reasonably tolerant companion.

I will go further.

It is not the birthdays *per se* which have caused me such discomfort, it is the necessity of purchasing presents which I have found so damnable.

No sooner has the wretched thing been handed over at the breakfast table than one is compelled to enter once more the nauseous and time-consuming palaver of thinking of a suitable gift for the next birthday.

It would not be irksome if the lady wife were to show even a modicum of gratitude for my offering.

'Oh, crumbs, not another one?' is her customary reaction. 'Why can't you think of something original for a change?'

Well, what she fails to appreciate is that the shop at Lords does not have an inexhaustible supply of novelties.

Dear God, she already has three different versions of the Gubby Allen toilet bag, and I simply refuse to pay out good money in purchasing yet another Alec Bedser pyjama case.

Stubbornly and steadfastly the lady wife refuses to

believe that the Ken Higgs autograph negligees and the gift-wrapped bottles of Eau de Washbrook are invariably snapped up by the MCC committee members long before the shop opens for its summer season.

How different it would all be if my wife were not to have birthdays.

How different indeed it would be if no one were to have birthdays, if life were to become a 'timeless test', if we were to be spared the death and decay which comes to all from the relentless passing of the years.

Would the world not be a better place today if Jack Hobbs were still wielding his silken willow, our city streets still rang to the echoes of carthorse hooves clopping on preening cobbles, and Mr 'Stainless' Stephen still tickled our chuckle muscles on our faithful cat's whisker?

Would not life be richer today if Spofforth and 'W. G.' were still engaged in mortal combat and the endless sunshine of 'The Golden Age' lit up in its radiance the bleakness and despair of this age of cold war, nancy boys and aluminium bats?

But no, dear friends, these are but the pipedreams of an old man.

Let us be happy with what we have.

I look now with surprising affection on the lady wife as she sits in our oak-timbered drawing room, her needles flashing in the flames of the log fire as she knits yet another set of nets for Mr Alf Gover's indoor cricket school.

And I think to myself – grow old in your own time, my dear.

Let the silver mingle with the gold.

Let us give succour and comfort to each other as our innings draws inexorably to its close.

But when you next have a birthday, for pity's sake let it be on the second day of Minor Counties versus Indian Tourists.

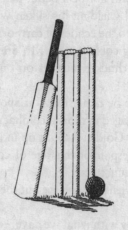

7
The Groundsman's Horse

During the course of a long and happy life one emotion has remained in my heart unfailingly and unflinchingly in the face of all the dangers and horrors that Mother Nature could throw at me – hurricane, typhoon, earthquake, war, famine, the cricket reports of Mr Tony Lewis.

The emotion is this:

An undying love for all our 'dumb friends'.

Thus it is that over the years I have cast my vote loyally and consistently for the Conservative and Unionist Party.

Thus it is that I send anonymously a bag of carrots each week to the BBC for the personal consumption of

Mr Raymond Brooks-Ward.

Thus it is, too, that I have steadfastly maintained my membership of The Tiger Tim Appreciation Society and been unstinting in my admiration for that great and noble statesman, philosopher, Olympic athlete and England opening bat, wicket-keeper and fast bowler, Lord Mountbatman of Burma.

It is the mention of Burma which reminds me of an episode in my life pertaining to our 'dumb friends', which even now many, many years later brings a glow of pride and feelings of the deepest satisfaction.

I was in Burma in the company of my father, who at the time was acting as adviser to the colonial administration during a particularly tricky outbreak of sight-screen desecration among the hill tribes of the Shan Plateau.

They were worrying times.

The Shans were seeking to impose their own version of the lbw rule on the loyal population of the towns and villages, and there were dark reports of the harassment of umpires and baggage masters in inaccessible valleys, over which MCC had only the most tenuous of influence.

My father, however, was a sanguine man.

Years of service in the farthest outposts of the British Empire had taught him that only the basest of savages, the most primitive of barbarians would fail to respond to the blandishments of a peace party of I Zingari mercenaries, who would play a ceremonial limited-over match with the dissidents and distribute to the masses free supplies of bakelite statuettes of Mr E.R. Dexter.

The efficacy of his philosophy had been proved time

and time again in the harsh experience of 'action in the field'.

Indeed at that time the only remaining pocket of resistance to MCC rule in the whole of the British Empire existed in remote islands of the Cocos group and certain recalcitrant city states in the West Riding of Yorkshire.

So it was that as we strolled through that Burmese town basking in the full and gentle bloom of a simpering spring afternoon there was a confident lilt to my father's tread and the faintest whisper of a smile upon his face.

He was happily recounting to me stories of early days spent on active service with The Royal Burma Frontier Scouts ('Plum' Warner's Own) when of a sudden he stopped dead in his tracks

His eyes widened.

His lower lip sagged.

And he exclaimed:

'Good God, laddie, look at that.'

I followed the direction of the pointing forearm.

And there a most singular sight struck my youthful eyes.

A broken-backed nag, head bowed, ribs protruding through scabrous flesh, matted fetlocks slouching through tropic dust, was plodding wearily down the centre of the pockmarked highway.

At its head was an emaciated figure in scarecrow rags, his bare feet blistered and scarred, his unkempt beard straggling over a hollow, naked chest and his sunken cheeks engrimed by the dust and dirt of years of neglect.

My father forthwith grasped my hand firmly and, striding purposefully across the street, placed himself forcefully in front of the horse and man.

'Whoa!' he bellowed.

Horse and man stopped, although neither raised its head.

'It isn't? It can't be,' said my father, and slowly and carefully he encircled the two wretched figures, his eyes narrowed, his brow furrowed.

Then he exclaimed:

'By jingo, it is. It's the groundsman's horse from Swanton St George.'

The effect of my father's words on the horse's attendant was remarkable to behold.

A choked gurgle came to his throat.

His bloodshot eyes rolled in their deep black sockets.

His knees began to tremble and suddenly he collapsed to the ground in a dead swoon.

I moved forward, but my father drew me back.

'Leave him be,' he shouted.

I froze in my tracks.

Silence.

My father clicked his tongue and swatted his thigh with the quarter-sized, bullet-scarred Strutt and Parker cricket bat he carried with him everywhere as protection against mosquitoes and my beloved mother's bad temper.

He was motionless for what seemed to me an eternity (almost as long as an innings by Mr Trevor Bailey, I was to think much later).

Then, wrinkling his nose, he extended his right leg and with the toe of his boot turned over the poor wretch who was still lying on the ground in the deepest of faints.

I gasped.

It was a white man.

My father grunted to himself with evident satisfaction.

Then he turned his attention to the pitiful nag which stood by his side, swatting its emaciated rump with a threadbare tail, vainly trying to keep at bay the attentions of the legions of flies which swarmed about its various orifices in a cloying, buzzing black mass like a clutch of animated eccles cakes.

My father nodded.

'Yes, by thunderation, it is the groundsman's horse,' he said, 'And I shall prove it to you forthwith.'

And with that he threw back his head and roared in a stentorian voice:

'Heavy roller!'

The effect was instantaneous.

The horse laid its ears flat against its skull, drew back its lips to reveal a set of yellowing and splintered teeth, and quite without warning lowered its head, lashed out with its back feet and set off at a canter down the dusty road, bucking and whinnying for all the world like Mr Ian Chappell appealing for lbw against Miss Rachel Heyhoe-Flint.

My father nodded again.

'That proves it conclusively,' he said. 'It always was shy of hard work with the roller.'

The horse did not travel far.

Such was the parlous nature of its condition that after twenty yards it ceased its mad flight and stood in the shade of a Robertson-Glasgow tree, wheezing and panting, its flanks shaking uncontrollably.

My father arranged for both horse and attendant to

be transported to our bungalow.

There in the stables in the shade of the giant Johnstonian oaks and the brooding Fingleton palms they were fed and watered and bedded down for the night in warm, clean hay.

It took a week for both to recover, and then my father was to learn from the groundsman (for thus was the identity of the poor wretch who had collapsed before his feet) the true story of their banishment to a land so different from the lush greensward and billowing beeches of their native Swanton St George.

Apparently the groundsman's horse had long been a feared institution at the village cricket team.

A fierce, uncontrollable brute, it obeyed only the commands of the groundsman, Festering, a sly and sullen lout of a man with a nose like a wicket-keeper's thumb.

It was allowed to graze unhindered on the village cricket pitch.

Such was its ill temper and ferocity that its presence was not removed even during the progress of matches.

No one dared approach it save for the groundsman, and thus a local rule was established: if the ball hit the horse, wheresoever it was standing, a four was awarded.

Most visiting teams were prepared to accept this condition, and all went well until the arrival of an Australian touring team, the Marsupials.

The Antipodean wanderers were skippered by Warren Croaker, who was later to achieve cricketing immortality by beating to death an umpire, with whose decision he disagreed (a practice much favoured by later generations of Australian Test cricketers).

Croaker was tried, convicted and sentenced to be executed by firing squad.

Dressed in flannels, pads and typical 'baggy' cap he was bound to the sight-screen at the Adelaide Oval and shot by a detachment of The Third Battalion Sam Loxton Dragoons.

His last words as he lay dying were reported to have been:

'Thank God, I was wearing my box.'

However, I digress.

Back to the match, Swanton St George versus The Marsupials.

The visitors from 'Down Under' took first knock and quickly amassed the staggering total of 239.

Swanton St George commenced their innings and were soon in 'the deepest trouble' at thirty-four for eight.

Certain defeat stared them in the face (to use the immortal and memorable words of that undisputed doyen of cricket writers, Mr E. R. Dexter).

It was at this moment that the groundsman, Festering, appeared at the wicket.

At once the wheels of the score-box began to whirr as, to use the expression of our Antipodean cousins from across the seas, the 'curator' struck four after four after four off his opponents' bowling.

But one thing was strikingly obvious – each of his fours was gained by the ball's hitting the grazing horse.

Slowly but surely the Swanton St George total approached the forbidding total set by their guests, the descendants of convicts, murderers and de-frocked members of MCC.

The 200 was reached when a ball smitten by Festering struck the horse a sickening blow on the left off paston.

The 220 was reached by the ball's hitting the heedless nag a resounding smack on a rump, the size of which was only exceeded many years later by the posterior portions of Mr M. C. Cowdrey.

It was then that (to borrow once more the sublime prose of Mr E. R. Dexter) 'excitement reached fever pitch'.

One over to go. Fifteen runs required.

Partnering Festering was the padre of the village, the Rev. Marchling-Thumper, who was later to become private chaplain to *The Sporting Chronicle*.

He was facing the bowling of the Australian skipper, Croaker.

The first delivery he received struck him a blistering blow in the ribcage.

'Run, you sod,' bellowed Festering.

The clerical gent scampered breathlessly to the bowler's end, glowering darkly at Festering, whose ill-chosen words had so offended his frail and delicate spirit.

One run gained. Fourteen to go.

It was then that spectators noticed a most singular occurrence – the groundsman's horse was approaching nearer and nearer to the wicket.

More singular still, it was actually beginning to move in the direction of each ball struck by Festering.

One four.

Two fours.

A wild swipe that did not connect.

A two, when a 'Chinese drive' flashed over first slip.

One ball to go. Four runs needed for victory.

Croaker polished the ball on his gin-stained flannels, glowering the while out of the corner of his eyes at the groundsman's horse.

He bowled.

Festering struck out.

The ball travelled no more than five feet on the off side.

The Australians cried out jubilantly.

Surely no more than a single could be obtained from the stroke?

But no.

The groundsman's horse threw back its head, whinnied and galloping like a dervish through the crowded off-side field, butted the Australian backward point just as he was about to pounce on the ball.

The Antipodean fell to the ground, shattering his hip flask beyond redemption.

The horse with a wicked grin of triumph bent down and gently nuzzled the ball towards the umpire.

'Four,' yelled Festering. 'The ball touched the horse. We've won.'

There are no words to do justice to the uproar that followed.

Not even the combined efforts of the pens of Mr Tony Lewis, Mr E. R. Dexter and 'the Proust of cricket literature', Mr Robin Marlar, could bring it to life on the printed page.

Accusation was followed by counter-accusation.

Wild imprecations filled the gentle English country air.

Such was the vileness of the Australian oaths that the bells in the church belfry were shattered to smithereens, and the treasured statue of the Blessed St Tony Greig of the Sorrows was split from cravat to money belt.

Peace was only restored when the Rev. Marchling-Thumper, who had taken refuge in the communal cricket bag, emerged from his hiding place white and trembling and, in a sacerdotal voice reminiscent of the dulcet tones of Mr Bill Alley at his most pious, shouted:

'Stop. Stop, I beg you.'

The clerical gent pointed a wavering forefinger at the groundsman, Festering, who was placidly feeding to his horse liberal quantities of Grannie Sinfield's Home-Made Gloucester Fudge.

'There is your culprit,' said the cricketing prelate.

Instantly Festering was surrounded by players from both sides.

His arms were twisted, his ribs were pummelled and he was forced to confess.

His plot was simple, effective and fiendish – he had trained his horse to run after balls hit by him and allow them to strike its body.

Shame. Disgrace.

The skipper of the village team apologized profusely to Croaker.

The provision of eight firkins of prime Rae and Stoll-meyer dark English ale and seventeen local virgins was sufficient to assuage him.

The apologies were accepted.

And thus it was that Festering and his horse were banished in ignominy to far-off Burma.

And as they plodded up the gangplank to the steamer which was to take them from Southampton to Rangoon, a voice addressed to Festering piped up from the back of the crowd.

'Run, you sod,' it said.

The voice belonged to the Rev. Marchling-Thumper.

My father listened to the story with tears in his eyes.

'You have suffered enough,' he said to Festering. 'Now I shall give you peace. Now I shall lead you to a land where everything you desire will be granted to you.'

Within the week he had taken the groundsman and his horse to the rebellious regions of the Shan plateau.

The effect was amazing.

The Shan tribesmen, primitive and innocent as they were, had never in the whole of their lives seen such a creature.

They threw down their arms, abandoned their lbw mutiny, and within weeks had settled down to a life of peace and obedience.

Indeed such was their amazement at this strange creature which had come to their midst from lands thousands of miles across the oceans that they deified it immediately.

And to this day the creature is to be seen stuffed and standing in a place of honour in the chief township of the Shan plateau.

Although what happened to the groundsman's horse is still unknown.

8

Mendip-Hughes

There is an old adage unique to this beloved 'summer game' of ours: 'the hour findeth the man'.

How true.

How often have cricketers been plucked from obscurity, thrown into the harsh spotlight of fame and notoriety and thus 'found' themselves and emblazened their names gloriously and permanently in the panoply of cricket's hall of fame?

We recall the immortal Fuller Pilch, hoisted from the vast brooding fastness of Norfolk to become one of the towering legendary figures of his age.

We think of the great Frank Tyson, dragged from the mediocrity of county cricket to become 'the scourge' of

Australian batsmen with the ferocity of his fast bowling.

We think of David Steele, plucked from obscurity of leadership of the Liberal Party to don the noble sweater of England and face unflinchingly the might of Lilley and Thompson.

And we think, too, of Geoff Boycott, plucked from the vast brooding fastness, the mediocrity and the obscurity of a Michael Parkinson chat show to become one of the greatest accumulators of runs known to the modern game.

Such a man was the one-legged Somerset off-spinner, Mendip-Hughes.

Let me state my attitude to him without prevarication:

It is my firm opinion that he was the finest uniped never to represent his country at Test match level.

I believe, moreover, that it was only prejudice of the basest sort which kept from him the representative honours given to men, the number of whose appendages may have been superior, but the number of whose talents was most definitely inferior.

I have no time for prejudice of any sort.

Mendip-Hughes should have been selected solely on his merits as an off-spinner.

He was not a nigger.

He was not an oily Italian, a foul-smelling Argentinian or a typical cowardly, wife-beating, dishonest, hysterical, garlic-munching Frenchman.

There was no excuse whatsoever for the selectors' failure to grant him the England cap he so richly deserved.

And so I feel it is high time he was given his 'just desserts'.

With that in mind I have composed the following short monograph.

It is generally assumed by historians of the 'summer game' that Mendip-Hughes lost his left leg during the first German offensive on the Somme in 1915.

This is not the case.

At the time in question Mendip-Hughes would have been approaching his sixth birthday, and, despite considerable research through the military archives, I have found no evidence to suggest that the British Army employed in its front line soldiers of such tender years.

No.

Let us scotch that particular rumour here and now.

Let us instead hoist our flag unashamedly to the assertion that the missing left leg, with which we now deal, met its demise in a piano accident at Crewkerne.

Mendip-Hughes himself was always most reticent in discussing the exact nature of the incident.

Who shall blame him?

There is a regrettable tendency these days for what I call 'Public Nosey Parkering'.

Fed by the unceasing efforts of journalists, broadcasters and similar scum, the British public has developed an insatiable appetite for tittle-tattle of the most trivial nature concerning people who for one reason or the other happen to be 'in the limelight'.

What possible interest can it be to know that E. W. Swanton wears maroon corduroy underpants and has in his study the complete collection of the records of Billy J. Kramer and the Dakotas?

Is the world a better place for knowing that despite all the evidence to the contrary Mr Robin Marlar is a thoroughly nice man?

Are we uplifted in soul and spirit by the knowledge that, despite his constant protestations, Mr Ned Sherrin did indeed once play rugby league football for Rochdale Hornets? – the match in which Miss Caryl Brahms was sent 'for an early bath' for butting an opponent.

No, let us draw a veil over Mendip-Hughes's unfortunate accident and say nothing about his mother's appalling carelessness in keeping a loaded Japanese blunderbuss in the piano stool and a Snoad and Hazelhurst Patent Poachers' Anti-Personnel Trap under the lid of the piano.

Let us concentrate on the influences which shaped the future distinguished career of Mendip-Hughes.

From the outset he was determined that regardless of his pedicular deficiency he would be 'Like all the other chaps'.

This indeed he was.

Like all boys of his age and background he became an accomplished player of the banjole, an expert in the early works of Krafft-Ebing, a most proficient translator into English of the writings of Mr E. W. Swanton, and winner in 1930 of the world's first one-legged ping-pong championship when he beat the Dane, Lars Erik Mortensen, 21-7 in the final set.

A brilliant career in diplomacy, banking, the university or wholesale greengrocery seemed assured to him.

Then came the untimely and catastrophic collapse of the family fortunes in 1931.

The painful details of this incident are best left covered in the mists of time.

What right have we to shake off the dust of faded memory and expose once more to public gaze the abject humiliation of Mendip-Hughes *père* with the collapse of his Surinam Steam Laundry Company and the subsequent allegations of forged banknotes, bribery, black magic and gross sexual impropriety?

That is voyeurism of 'the worst sort' and is best left to those pedlars of filth and gossip, whose livings are earned feasting on the carrion of others' misfortunes.

Let us return to poor Mendip-Hughes, penniless, without prospects and cast adrift with the MCC Cricketing Freaks, which toured the world in 1933.

The party was led by Mr M. P. Bradwell-Jackson, the short-sighted Oxfordshire wicket-keeper, who was later to achieve cricketing immortality in 1956 by proposing marriage to Mr K. D. 'Slasher' Mackay of Queensland and Australia during tea interval at the Cheltenham Festival.

The tour was an outstanding success.

There were notable victories over a Turkish Transvestites Eleven, a Peruvian Onanists Select, and a most exciting tied match with the Bondage and Nude Bicycling Gymkhana of Bombay.

For Mendip-Hughes, however, the tour meant nothing but misery and despair and frustration.

He was constantly no-balled in Tibet.

He had trouble with his run up in Brazzaville.

His cricket bag was eaten by spectators in Borneo.

It was not until the final match of the tour, a three-day contest against Twelve Amputees of Arabia, that a chink of light appeared in the tunnel of gloom and darkness.

Mendip-Hughes was 'spotted' by a member of the committee of the Somerset County Cricket Club who, as luck would have it, was serving a brief spell as Director General Royal Ablutions to the Sultan of Oman.

This perspicacious gentleman immediately tele-graphed Taunton, and within the month Mendip-Hughes had joined the county of the winged dragon to embark upon a career that was as dazzling as it was brief.

There is no need for me to dwell on his deeds on the cricket fields.

No one who saw him is ever likely to forget that distinctive bound and hop to the wicket, that jack-in-the-box spring as he released the ball, that strangled, tortured cry as he leapt one-legged high into the air to appeal to the umpire.

Let us rather concentrate on his subsequent career off the field, over which totally unjustifiable clouds of sus-picion and calumny have been cast.

Let us destroy once and for all the vile rumour that Mendip-Hughes's sudden disappearance from the crick-et scene in August 1936 was the result of 'an incident' with the groundsman's horse at Wells.

One has only to read that sadly neglected volume, *The Pensées of Horace Hazell*, to be given 'the true story'.

Suffice it to say that even at the time I myself was convinced that the horse's undoubted distress had more to do with its purloining and subsequent consumption of Harold Gimblett's jock strap than any mis-demeanour on the part of Mendip-Hughes.

The reasons for the sudden retirement of Mendip-Hughes are more fascinating and compelling than that.

For the first time, freed from the constrictions of the Official Secrets Act, I can reveal that on that fateful day at Wells Mendip-Hughes was summoned to 'higher things'.

He was called to the service of King and country to establish in M15 its first Cricket Section.

For many months previously secret service chiefs and their political masters had been eyeing the activities of Nazi Germany and Fascist Italy with considerable suspicion.

It was, I believe, the uniform opinion of those august gentlemen that Herr Hitler and Signor Mussolini could only be described as stinkers and out-and-out rotters.

This opinion was born out many years later by Germany's vile and wanton destruction of the cricket pavilion at Old Trafford, and the totally unprovoked attack by incendiary bombs and parachute aerial mines on the Farmer White Home for Retired Leg Spinners at Keating St Rodda.

Accordingly they conceived the daring and novel notion that, if clandestine relationships could be established in Germany and Italy with people of a cricketing bent, a popular uprising could be engendered which would sweep away forever the odious dictatorships and restore in their place a free society, in which the jack boot would be replaced by the cricket boot and the rhino whip would give way to the Gunn and Moore three-springer.

It was not for want of industry or courage that Mendip-Hughes failed to bring their plans to fulfilment.

Despite a natural and totally justifiable dislike of his colleagues in M15, a loathesome collection of nancy boys and ladies with loud voices and hairy chests, Mendip-Hughes threw himself into his new job with enthusiasm and a reckless disregard for his own safety.

It is not generally known that Mendip-Hughes narrowly escaped death in 1938 when he was arrested in Berlin and charged with the illegal distribution of cricket balls, which he had brought into the country concealed in the false bottom of a cricket bag.

Few people, I am certain, are aware that Mendip-Hughes only narrowly failed to persuade Count Ciano to bring a representative eleven of his black shirts to play Mr H. D. G. Leweson-Gower's Eleven at the Scarborough Festival of 1939.

In the same year Mendip-Hughes achieved the triumph of inducing Reichsmarschall Hermann Goering and his wife to attend the Saturday of the Lords Test.

No blame can be attached to him for the fact that when the time came there were no tickets available, and the obese Hum and his odious spouse were compelled to spend the afternoon at Buckingham Palace playing three-card brag with Queen Mary and Princess Alice of Athlone.

One can only conjecture sadly about how different the fate of the world would have been, had this and other enterprises been granted with success.

Alas, it was not to be.

Neither was Mendip-Hughes to be granted further opportunity to exercise his talents, for war was declared shortly after Goering's return to his native heath and our hero was straightway plunged into the nefarious world of intrigue and espionage.

Very few details remain concerning the termination of his career with M15.

We do know that during the war he made several dangerous and arduous missions to occupied Europe.

We know that on his last mission he was parachuted into Vichy France early in the spring of 1943.

From this he did not return.

No one is sure of the exact nature of his fate. However, one interesting fact has recently come to light.

There has been discovered a small and remote village in the heart of the Auvergne, in which the men to this very day play cricket.

Even more fascinating is the fact that they play cricket on one leg.

It would be comforting to think that this is the legacy Mendip-Hughes left to posterity, although it must be pointed out that Mendip-Hughes played cricket on his right leg, while the men of the Auvergne play on their left leg.

Let us be charitable and state that this is yet another example of the entrenched Gallic obstinacy when faced with the noble culture and moral values of England.

9
Cricketers' Cook Book

In my experience, cricketers and all those associated with our beloved 'summer game' are without exception outstanding trenchermen.

I recall Nuttall, the Lancashire professional, who once ate half a carthorse during the luncheon adjournment in a match against Leicestershire.

He claimed he would have eaten the whole of the horse, had the bridle not stuck in his teeth.

I remember Sumpter, a drinking man of heroic proportions who once drank ten quarts of claret and a can of linseed oil before going out to bat against Gentlemen of Ulster (they could only find five, incidentally).

He is the only man in history as having been given out:

'Drunk hit wicket and umpire.'

With this in mind I have collected a few favourite recipes of cricketers both famous and humble, and these I present for your delectation and edification.

Alec Bedser's Fancy

Alec Bedser writes:

'I like incredibly boring food.

'And so does my brother.

'I like sausages and chips. I think this is the most incredibly boring food I know.

'And so does my brother.

'When you are making sausages and chips, the first thing to do is to buy the ingredients.

'This is quite easy.

'First of all you go to the butcher's with your brother, and you say:

' "A pound of sausages, please."

'The butcher will probably say:

' "Certainly, sir, what sort do you require?"

'You answer:

' "Pork, please."

'The butcher will in all likelihood then reply:

' "Can't I tempt you with the beef, sir? They are highly recommended."

'You reply:

' "Pork, please."

'His next tack will be to say:

' "What about the herb sausages, sir?"

'You reply:

' "Pork, please."

'If he should then go on to say:

' "The tomato-flavoured are very delicious, sir."

'You reply:

' "Pork, please."

'Next you go to the greengrocer's.

'And so does your brother.

'You say to the greengrocer:

' "Five pounds of potatoes, please."

'The greengrocer will in all probability say:

' "Certainly, sir. What variety do you require – King Edwards, Lincolnshire red, waxy whites, Pentland Squire or Pembrokeshire new?"

'You reply:

' "I don't give a shit."

'After this you go home.

'And so does your brother.

'Now it gets even more incredibly boring.

'You have to cook it.

'Usually I don't bother.

'I let my brother do it.'

My dear, dear friend, Robert Carrier, is not only a noted gourmet and epicure, he is also something of a cricket fanatic.

What happy memories I have of enchanting weekends spent at his bewitching country home.

All those lovely young men arrayed in flannels and silk shirts of purest white disporting themselves on the cricket field, while dear Bob tirelessly and selflessly worked in the kitchen chopping up the pickled onions for the post-match hot-pot supper.

What bliss.

On my last visit to his home he set before me a magnificent display of some of his favourite cakes and puddings.

This is my report on them:

Arlott Cake. A rich, fruity concoction. Aromatic and deeply satisfying to the soul. A cake to linger over on long, brooding winter evenings. A cake to eat with vintage port. Scrumptious.

Swanton Pudding. A heavy, suet-based confectionary which I found intimidating and indigestible. It turned the custard lumpy.

Keating Krackle. A delicious, spicey biscuit. A little too eager to please, perhaps, but full of subtlety and delicate flavour. Delicious accompaniment to the incomparable Cook and Wells Gloucester country cider.

Auntie Lewis's Welsh Tart. An over-fussy dessert. Looks all right on the outside, but its flavour is inconsequential and its texture is irritatingly bland.

Jonner's Jam Sandwich. A jolly cake full of fun and hearty flavour. Marvellous for tuck boxes and midnight feasts in the dorm.

Marlar Melting Moments. Made me fart all night.

Blofeld Gateau. A blend of choice and exotic fruits from all parts of the world. Much beloved by BBC commentators. Used by Bill Frindall as a paper weight and as a gag to silence Trevor Bailey.

It might surprise those who have visited my home to learn that the lady wife 'on her day' is quite a decent cook – if you like that sort of thing.

Here are are a few of her favourite dishes:
Duckworth a l'orange
Fishlock pie
Brain with braund and cranston sauce
Pridgeon pie
Roast tim lamb with tom graveny
Insole colbert
Appleyard and bobberry pie
Bannerjee curry a la modi with clive rice
Cecil parkin
Dilley con carne
Jellied ealham
Rabone steak
Winston Place and chips
Van Geloven-ready chicken
Jardines on toast
Pleass pudding
Todd in the hole
Fagg roll

Finally, I invited several well-known 'personalities' from our 'summer game' to tell their idea of the perfect meal and the perfect day to accompany it.

Here are some of their replies:

Freddie Trueman
'My idea of the perfect meal is as follows: it would be in a discreet, candlelit Bloomsbury vegetarian restaurant in the company of Margaret Drabble, Marghanita Laski, Iris Murdoch and Jill Tweedie.'

E. R.Dexter

'I can think of nothing more perfect than an evening spent in the company of my very dear friend, Michael Parkinson, in his home town of Burnley.

'After a delicious meal of beans on toast in the bus station café we would repair to the vaults bar of the Queens Hotel and there swap yarns about happy days at our respective prep schools, about carefree, languid, summer afternoons spent on punts among the dreaming spires of our alma maters and of the fun we had as young subalterns during our National Service.

'After that it would be a night dancing the hours away at the Civic Ballroom, Hoyland Common, in the company of Janet Street-Porter and Russell Harty.'

Majid Khan (brother of the well-known songwriter, Sammy)

'It's well known that I'm a sociable sort of bloke. I'd like nothing better than a night on the batter in Cardiff with the boys. I'd ring them all up – Wilf, Eifion, 'Lol', Alan, Nashy, 'Lofty' Pete Walker and all the other boozy old wankers – and I'd say: "Come on, boys, on with your drinking boots. The treat's on me."

'Then we'd get stuck into pints of Brain's Dark at The Old Arcade. Then it'd be across to Canton to give the old "Skull Attack" a bloody good thrashing.

'Then we'd get a cab and hot foot it down Tiger Bay for a good old arse-rattling curry. Then we'd all piss off back to Tony Cordle's and bugger up his Vivaldi records.'

Geoffrey Boycott

'I should throw open my official residence to a small and select group of my closest friends and admirers.

'Among those present would be: Sir Keith Joseph, Sir Geoffrey Howe, Professor Milton Keynes, Simon Rattle, Snoo Wilson, Vanessa Redgrave, Sir Arnold and Lord Goodman, Lady Antonia Frazier and her brother, Joe, Sir Cecil Beaton, Larry Olivier, Sir Douglas Bader, Sir Isiah Berlin, Mr Barry Took, Victor Gollancz, Sir George Weidenfeld and his wife, Mavis Nicholson, Queen Salote of Tonga, Senator Edward Kennedy, Lord Lucan and Miss Kitty McShane, Miss Jan Leeming, Mr Ned Sherrin, Mr Barry Cryer, Mr John Junkin, Mr Robin Bailey and his father, Trevor, Dame Petula Clark, Cliff Richard, and in contrast from the world of music, Miss Elizabeth Schwarzkopf and Miss Ann Shelton, Patrick Moore, Mr Brian Clough, Andrew Lloyd-Webber, John Julius Northwich, Lord David Cecil, Lord Carrington, the Duke of Kent, Mr Harry Pilling, Auberon Waugh and his daughter, Evelyn, Hinge and Brackett, Sir Michael Edwardes (who's small enough to come twice) and finally my mentor and dearest confidant, the one man I consider to be even greater than I at this moment in time, Mr Peter West and his mother, Dame Rebecca.

'After taking a net we would all repair to my state apartments where I would deliver the annual Sir Geoffrey Boycott Memorial Lecture, which I give every year.

'Then after taking another net and having a rub down by Bernard Thomas we would retire to the state dining rooms, where individual fish and ship suppers would be provided by Mr Harry Ramsden.

'Then after taking another net we would all have after-dinner mints like you see them doing on the television adverts.

'I wonder if I should have invited Ray Illingworth?'

Alec Bedser
'What I'd like most is an incredibly boring evening at home with my brother and a plate of sausage and chips.'

10
Polar Games

In my opinion a vast amount of unmitigated tosh, piffle and utter drivel has been written about the enmity and antipathy which existed between the two polar explorers, Scott and Amundsen.

Jealousy, hatred, deep, brooding resentment, sheer bloody-mindedness: all these emotions played their part in the intense hostility which existed between those two men.

But what caused these feelings?

Conventional canon has it that Scott's detestation of Amundsen was the direct result of the Norwegian's cheating and entering into a race for the South Pole.

Absolute balderdash.

The whole can of worms was created by one event and one event alone – a cricket match played at Cape Evans in Antarctica on 18 September 1911, between elevens representing the respective polar expeditions of Captain Scott and Roald Amundsen.

It was the ill feeling engendered by this match which caused all the subsequent virulence of passions and ultimately, in my view, the untimely death of Scott himself.

For more than fifty years this incident has been 'hushed up' by those jealous to preserve Scott's reputation as an heroic figure whose death in the snowy wastes of Antarctica was a lasting monument to the typical English qualities of manly virtue, moral courage and noble self-sacrifice.

At the same time these misguided men sought to portray Amundsen as a base and treacherous liar, a glory hunter and, above all, a cheat and a practioner of gamesmanship of the 'very worst sort'.

The facts prove otherwise.

Let them now speak for themselves.

As I sit in my study now with the lapwings wheeling and diving above the water meadows, the fat black rooks purring in the vicarage elms and the milkman's horse ambling heavily down the honeysuckled lane for all the world like Tom Goddard plodding back to his mark at Cheltenham, my mind wanders back in time, soaring weightlessly over storm-thrashed oceans, gliding gracefully over gnashing floes of ice and silent wastes of dazzling snow.

And like a great brooding skua it skims down tumbling mountain ramparts, cascading ice falls and lumbering glaciers and alights on a broken-backed wooden crate, and its glinting steely eyes survey the scene.

A hut.

Scott's hut at Cape Evans.

Scott's specially constructed hut with its score-box, its balconies for home side and visitors side, its separate entrances for gentlemen and players and the broad sweep of its long room windows.

And outside on the snow a hive of activity.

Two ponies pulling a heavy roller.

The unmistakeable figure of Petty Officer Evans erecting a sight-screen.

Captain Oates in the nets bowling his distinctive leg breaks and googlies to Lieutenant Bowers.

(How curious, incidentally, and how felicitous that Oates should share the same Christian name initials as the celebrated Kent and England wicket-keeper, Mr Leslie Ames.)

Let us not dwell on that matter, however.

Let us direct our gaze to the broad expanse of snow shining and white and pure outside Scott's hut.

Do you see?

Chief Stoker Lashly digging a popping crease and Cecil Meares feeding the remnants of a matting wicket to his beloved huskies.

All is ready for the historic match.

But wait.

Let us examine the circumstances which created this most significant event in the whole history of polar exploration.

I have in my possession documentary evidence to

prove beyond peradventure that Scott had known of Amundsen's intention to strike out for the South Pole for at least one year.

Indeed discussions and meetings had taken place between the two men at Nansen's home in Christiana.

It was at the last of these meetings that Scott came up with a proposition that was as novel as it was daring.

The two expeditions should set out for Antarctica, he suggested.

But once there they should play a cricket match.

The winners of this match would be the expedition which would strike out for the Pole.

Despite his unfamiliarity with the 'summer game', Amundsen enthusiastically accepted the challenge.

With typical Norwegian thoroughness he threw himself into the meticulous planning which was essential if the polar cricket match was to be won.

We know from the archives that in the summer of 1910 Amundsen secretly brought a party of Norwegians to Lords to be given instruction in the rudiments of cricket.

During this time Amundsen took his expert ski maker, Bjaaland, to the factories of Messrs Gunn and Moore to learn the mysteries of the time-honoured craft of cricket bat-making.

I am aware that there are academic historians with their foul-smelling socks and damp handshakes who will hotly dispute these assertions of mine.

'Fiddle de dee,' they will say. 'There was no arrangement.'

Oh, really?

Well, consider, my friends, the case of Trygve Gran.

He was Norwegian, yet he was a member of Scott's party. Why?

Historians state that Scott engaged Gran as skiing instructor to the expedition. But we know from diaries that Gran was scarcely ever employed in that capacity.

The so-called 'experts' have spent decades wondering why. Indeed a recent biographer of Scott and Amundsen has suggested that Gran's inactivity was one of the many blunders committed by Scott in his running of the ill-fated expedition.

What arrant nonsense.

Gran's role in the polar expedition in the light of our knowledge of the cricket match is blindingly obvious.

He was to be umpire.

Scott with typical English sportsmanship had decided that the umpire his team would provide would be Norwegian.

So are gestures purely altruistic in motive twisted and distorted for the sake of cheap 'sensationalism'.

Let us no longer detain ourselves with such perfidy and concentrate our attentions on the match itself.

Unfortunately, the score-book is no longer extant.

By an extreme and profoundly irritating stroke of fate it was in the hip pocket of Captain Oates when he set off on his final and heroic last journey into the polar night and eternal oblivion.

Would that he had only paused a second before opening the flap of that snowbound tent.

Would that he had considered the full implications of his dramatic gesture.

Had he done so, I am convinced that there is not the slightest doubt he would have handed over that precious score-book to his companions and would thus have been accorded by posterity even greater warmth than he now holds in our affections. Oates was indeed 'a very gallant gentleman' – but he was also damnably inconsiderate.

Another sad gap in our knowledge of this match is caused by the absence of score-cards.

We know from his diaries that Dr Edward 'Bill' Wilson illustrated in watercolour several of these cards, which were printed on the portable press specially shipped out to the Antarctic for this purpose.

Indeed the workings of this press had been a major and constant source of concern to Scott over the months of detailed planning he had made into the running of the expedition.

He had, in fact, 'borrowed' one of the score-card printing presses from Lords and in the winter of 1910 taken it to Arctic Norway for special ice trials.

It had failed dismally, but with a stubbornness of spirit that was ultimately to prove his undoing Scott refused to listen to advice and insisted on bringing to the Antarctic a score-card printing press that was known to be a failure in the extremely low temperatures prevailing in that inhospitable clime.

Would that he had taken a press from Old Trafford.

Would, too, that we were able to solve the mystery of the 'missing' cards.

Theories for their loss abound.

The most likely is, I believe, the one which maintains that Scott took the score-cards with him on his final dash to the pole, intending to leave them buried in a casket at the South Pole itself to prove to the world (if proof were needed) the cultural and moral supremacy of England.

On reaching the pole and discovering that Amundsen had been there before him, Scott was devastated.

In a fit of pique he took the score-cards from the container carried on a halter round the neck of Petty Officer Evans and, ripping them to shreds with his teeth, hurled them high into the sky to be whisked away by the polar gales and buried forever in the snowy deserts, which were later to entomb him and his companions with fatal results.

No, we have no 'facts and figures' about the match, and so we must rely on the diaries and letters of those who were present.

We know, for example, from his diaries that Scott had been brooding with deep misgivings about the match for many months after the departure of the *Terra Nova* from England.

He wrote:

'Everything that could be done to ensure the success of our party has been done. We are a fine body of men, resolute in purpose, steadfast in spirit. Our equipment is the finest that could be devised. We have ponies, tractors and dogs. We have men trained in every facet of the scientific skills. We have old polar hands who have experienced every one of the unimaginable hardships and terrors that mother nature will hurl at us. Yet one nagging doubt remains – where is our off-spinner and where is our second change seamer?'

Others, too, had their fears.

Oates writing to his mother in his typical graphic and unpunctuated style said:

'We are a pretty dismal lot we are all willing but where is the leadership? We have absolutely no experience of cricket in polar regions, yet Scott refuses point blank to organize decent nets, and what infuriates me even more is that we have on board *Terra Nova* a biologist name of Lillie. He's a fast bowler of rare old promise yet Scott with typical idocy refuses to allow him to join the shore party. Madness.'

Madness? Stubborness?

Or was Scott by deliberately refusing the services of a man who was to become one of the greatest fast bowlers the 'summer game' has ever know, showing manifestations of the propensity for self-destruction which would later end with such tragic results?

Even Bowers – loyal, uncomplaining, hard-working gallant little 'Birdie' Bowers – had his misgivings.

When he saw Amundsen and his team arrive at Cape Evans for the match, he wrote to his mother:

'Scott is a topper – a better leader or tent companion one could not have. I can say unhesitatingly tht he is one of the best – an absolute sahib. But when I look at the gear and the togs the Norwegians have brought for the match, I admit the old heart plummets right to the boots.'

Those words were prophetic indeed.

The Norwegians' equipment was certainly impressive

Specially prepared wax for their skis and cricket bats, quick-release bindings for their cricket pads, extra-long, non-corrosive crampons for their cricket boots, and warm comforting reindeer-fur lining for their abdominal protectors – the Norwegians had 'done their homework'.

If that were not enough to cast a cloud over the minds of the English team, worse was to follow when a bitter dispute broke out betweeen Scott and Amundsen over the use of dogs and horses.

Scott had shipped out ponies especially for the pulling of the heavy roller.

Amundsen refused to allow that. He had brought his huskies, and he insisted that they be allowed to pull the heavy roller.

The argument raged.

Finally, it was agreed that trials should take place to test the relative merits of dog and pony.

Let Scott's diaries speak for themselves.

As he sat on the players' balcony of the hut at Cape Evans watching the ponies pulling the heavy roller he wrote:

'It is pathetic to see the ponies floundering in the soft patches. Now and again they have to stop, and it is horrid to see them half engulfed in the snow, panting and heaving from the strain.'

Amundsen's huskies, however, when put to the test, simply skimmed over the surface of the snow, the heavy roller whirring gaily in their wake.

Once more the months of meticulous preparation

had paid their dividends, for Amundsen had the previous winter spent four months with his dogs on the high, bleak snow plateaux of Telemark, training them to pull heavy roller and gang mower.

Scott never forgave Amundsen for this public humiliation, especially as at the end of the day together with Oates, Wilson, Bowers and Edgar Evans he was compelled to 'manhaul' the heavy roller.

Under those inauspicious circumstances it was not unexpected that Scott lost the toss.

'Bill' Wilson, his sturdy and steadfast confidant, tried hard to cheer him up, but he was inconsolable.

'I fear the worst, Bill,' he said. 'I fear we are done for.'

How apt his misgivings seemed as on the most perfect of wickets the Norwegians totted up a score of major proportions.

From the diary of 'Birdie' Bowers we know that he himself caught out Wisting from the bowling of Atkinson for seventy-eight.

We know, too, how to Scott's fury Gran turned down his lbw appeal against, chagrin of chagrin, his opposite skipper, Amundsen, who subsequently went on to score 175 – although some historians maintain that his score was, in fact, 174 owing to Gran's failure to signal a 'short run'.

We do not know the exact Norwegian score, although I suspect it was nearer to 600 than 700.

What we do know, however, is that as soon as Scott's Eleven went into bat they were stricken by the most appalling weather. Blizzards, gales, lashing hail storms and sub-zero temperatures turned the wicket into a real 'sticky dog', and in next to no time Scott's side, finding

Helmer Hanssen virtually unplayable, were in dire straits at 78 for 8 with Oates ret. hurt, bad feet.

It was at this moment that the ultimate tragedy occurred.

The weather closed in so badly that play was no longer possible. Day after day after day the vile polar weather did its worst.

Scott wrote in his diary:

'Dear God, this place is terrible. Worse by far than the Thursday of an Old Trafford Test.'

But worse was indeed to follow.

In the negotiations that had taken place before the match Scott had insisted that his expedition would be responsible for supplies.

Reluctantly Amundsen had agreed, but only on the condition that if supplies failed, Scott would forfeit the match.

Supplies began to run out.

The special depot built on the long leg boundary could not be reached owing to the severity of the weather, and stores in the hut began to run dangerously low.

On the fourth day the cucumber sandwiches ran out.

By the fifth day there was no egg and cress, and on the seventh day the last of the maids of honour was consumed.

With the tea urn dip stick no longer registering, Amundsen took action.

He demanded that either Scott replenish the stores by making an immediate dash to the long leg depot, or he would insist that the match be forfeited.

With the ponies useless for such a task Scott and his

four companions set out to man haul the sledge to the depot and its supplies of swiss rolls, pilchard paste and gentleman's relish.

The journey there and back took ten days – ten days of the most appalling hardships and deprivations which Scott and his gallant band bore with a courage that was almost superhuman.

But when they got back, Amundsen had gone – and he had claimed victory.

The next Scott was to hear of him was when he reached the South Pole and there found the flag of Norway flying from Amundsen's Gunn and Moore cricket bat.

It was the ultimate humiliation.

So there is 'the true story'.

For more than five decades it has been hushed up for one reason and one reason alone – the fact that Norway defeated England at cricket.

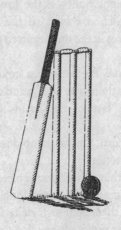

11

The Ones That Got Away

Just recently there has come into my possession a trunkful of priceless cricket memorabilia.

Among the many items of immeasurable and overpowering interest in this positive Pandora's chest of cricketing nostalgia are:

Mr D. R. Jardine's personal toenail clippers; a portion of Mr Peter West's left sock discovered in fossil remains in the BBC commentary box at Trent Bridge; a half-sucked Malteser, property of J. J. Warr Esq. (the other half, I believe is in the possession of The Trustees The Robin Marlar Appreciation Society, Car Park Attendants' Branch); and a first edition of the very rare E. W. Swanton book, *On The Hippy Trail to Katmandu*.

But of all the treasures the one which pleases me most is the dust-laden file, stained with Cooper's marmalade and Brown and Robertson's damson jam, which contains a series of obituaries, which, for one reason or another, never appeared in Wisden.

I propose to present to you an alphabetical selection of these sublimely precious examples of literature of the 'summer game'.

A 'Fong, Horace. Born Shanghai, June 1907. Considered by many to have been the finest Chinese left-handed opening bat of his generation. Leading member of the 'gang of four' who transformed Chinese cricket in the post Go AI Len era. Leader of the left-handed revolution in 1960s with I Kin, What Ton and Pull Ar. Executed Ba Cup 1969.

Bunch, Herbert Neville. Born Alston Junction, August 1878. Found dead on a train outside Tamworth (Low Level) station. He was wearing a fireman's helmet, sequined G-string and pink patent-leather dancing pumps.

Coats-Stufffley, Winston Foden. Born Gibson-beyond-Cardus, 17 October 1901. Hon. Sec. Faroes Cricket Society, 1932-37. Died at sea, 1929.

Dabson, Robert Falcon. Born Warrington, September 1888. Distinguished scorer and mountaineer. First man to make a single-handed ascent of the south face of the Warner Stand.

Evans, Gareth Dylan Gwynfor Mostyn Bismarck. Welsh cricket professional. Born Felinfoel, 1915. Died of drink Vale of Neath, 1931.

Fudge, Granville. Born May 1900. Forceful right-hand bat and fast medium left arm bowler. Played five seasons for Worcestershire. The only player ever to score three successive first-class centuries while wearing ladies underwear. Great friend of Bunch Herbert Neville (CV). Died Tangiers, 1975.

Golightly, Harriet. Born Christopher St Martins, July 1918. Sister of Ben Golightly, official scorecard printer to Queen Wilhemina Henrietta of the Netherlands. Ladies champion, Throwing the Cricket Ball, 1936-39. Accomplished contortionist. Died in a cricket bag, Fenners, 1943.

Hancock, Thomas. Born Marlborough, May 1786. Died London, March 1865. Inventor and manufacturer who founded the British rubber industry and thus gained the undying gratitude of countless generations of Australian cricket tourists to England. His chief invention, 'the masticator', worked rubber scraps into a shredded mass of rubber that could be worked into blocks or rolled into sheets. This process, perfected in 1821, led to a partnership with the Scottish chemist and inventor of waterproof fabrics, Charles Macintosh. The best known of the waterproof articles they produced were macintosh coats, popularly known as Mackintoshes. In his memory a statue was erected at the back of the Harry Makepeace Memorial Bicycle Sheds, Old Trafford.

Inkpen, Mervyn Alsager. Born Melbourne, March 1927. Doctor distinguished for his research into injuries resulting from the cricket field. Discoverer of 'off-spinners' hip' and 'Leg slips' hemmorroids'. Killed by falling sightscreen, Brisbane, 1957.

Jutter, Ernest Offenbach. Born Batavia 1918. Treasurer Musicians' Cricket Society, 1947-77. Composer of Ballet Suite, 'A Night with Nureyev, a Day with James Langridge.'

Kilknockin, Harry Montague Devenish, Third Earl of. Born Newport, IOW, November 1899. Wicket-keeper for Eton, Balliol, Gentlemen of Ireland and House of Lords Strollers. Maj. Gen. F. K. St J. L-B-W writes:
' "Stinky" Kilknockin achieved cricketing immortality with his unfailing, unbounding sense of humour, his ability to "stick to the task" whatever the cost and the constant and nauseous stench to his socks. I have no hesitation in stating that Kilknockin's socks were the most revolting objects I have encountered in a lifetime's devotion to the "summer game" and all matters pertaining. The cleanliness of teeth, too, left a "lot to be desired" and his nose was remarkable for the number of hairs protruding therefrom. His eating habits, too, were notorious for their loathesomeness and his sexual proclivities were detested by all those who had the misfortune to suffer from his attentions. He was also a "more than adequate" middle order batsman.'

Lugg, Bert. Born Arlott-by-Keating, February 1856. West country cricketing wit and raconteur. Author of *A Golden Treasury of Cricketing Parlance* and *John and Mary Whitehouse, A Warwickshire Romance*. Died 1949, Melford St Swantons.

Maharabhindi, Maharajah of. Friend and confidant of the great Earl Mountbatman, the man who captained England in 867 Test matches, scored the greatest number of first-class centuries, achieved 'the double' on no less than seventy-nine occasions, won the Ashes single-handedly with one great bound five times and was the father of Sir Jack Hobbs, Sir Donald Bradman and Mr B. D. 'Bomber'Wells. Also winner of 'Mastermind' on six successive occasions.

Newt, Hector Ian. Scottish cricketer. Born Peebles, 1906. Died Titmus, 1976.

O'Casey, Sean. Born Dublin, 30 March 1880. Irish playwright and enthusiast of the 'summer game'. Author of the two definitive cricket dramas, 'Juno and the Pocock', and 'Shadow of a Bradman'.

Ponting, Herbert G. Official photographer on all Sir Dereck Shackleton's expeditions to the polar regions. Famous for his pictures of the harrowing hardships suffered by all on the Dexter Expedition to West Indies, 1963. Illustrator of the Sainsbury and Horton edition of *The Ingoldsby-Mackenzie Legends*.

Quirck, Graham. Born Perth, 1928. Collapsed in the gents toilet during an interval in the match Western Australia versus Queensland, 1959, and when carried into the pavilion life was found to be extinct. Antipodean cricket correspondent for many years to *Exchange and Mart*. Joint Nobel Prize Winner for Scoring with Bill Frindall, 1958. Perspired excessively.

Rust, Sydney George. A well-loved and much-imitated

'character' for five decades at Bramall Lane. Lord Hawke writes: 'Rust was a capital fellow.'

Sellows-Hoffmann, Hugo Ralph. Born Trinidad, 1911. Architect of cricket pavilions. Designer of the unsinkable patrons bar, Hove (1937). Talented painter noted for his sight-screen *trompe l'oeils*. Of particular merit are his 'Madonna and Child opening the innings, Buxton' and his immortal 'The Purification of Binks, Headingley'.

Tattenhall, Clayton Geoffrey. Famous groundsman. Born Sowerbutts-in-Tyldesleydale, 1901. Breeder of the quick crop radish to be grown on Old Trafford pitches during rain-stopped-play intervals. Moved to Gloucester where he invented the moveable batting order now known as 'The Rotation of Crapps'.

U, Nu. See Nu, U.

Voigt, Conrad Arthur. Died on 9 January 1939, appeared 'a few times' in the Buckinghamshire Second Eleven. A good defensive batsman, he was particularly strong on the off side. W. W. H. writes: 'Voigt was a good defensive batsman, particularly strong on the off side.'

Xenophen. Greek philosopher. Died Attercliffe, 350 BC. Originator of the philosophy that only men of native birth may play for Yorkshire.

Yapp, Llewellyn. Welsh patriot. Born Pontyboyce, February 1902. Translator into Welsh of *Wisden's Almanack* and E.W. Swanton's *On The Hippy Trail to Pontymister*. Died of boredom during Mr Tony

Lewis's benefit year.

Zog, Albania, ex-King of. An absolute stinker. *See also* Tinniswood, Peter.

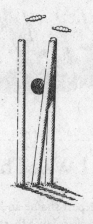

12

I Was There

It is with the deepest shame and sense of misery that I have to admit it – yes, I was there.

On the greatest day of infamy in our 'summer game' it was my profound misfortune to be present and, indeed, play a central part in the wretched proceedings which so marred and scarred the Saturday of the Centenary Test at Lords.

Let us be quite clear about one thing:

In no way do I condone the attitude of those spectators who abused and in some cases physically assaulted the two umpires on the steps of the pavilion.

While I have considerable sympathy with the views of those who maintain that anyone who has the effrontery to look like Mr Harold 'Dicky' Bird (or even to be Mr Harold 'Dicky' Bird) deserves to be given a thorough thrashing every morning of his life, I believe that these feelings should never be allowed public expression – especially at 'headquarters'.

While I believe, too, that the England captain, Mr Ian Botham, has the looks and the manner of a recently made redundant chef on a British Rail dining car, and that his Australian counterpart, Mr Ian Chappell, bears a remarkable resemblance to a cheroot-toting lieutenant colonel in some vile-smelling Central American republic, this gives no licence to express outright contempt towards them.

However, when all is said and done, and, although it pains me to the core of my soul to say it, on the day in question it is easy to understand and to forgive the baseness of behaviour of everyone concerned.

And it is even easier to point the finger at those responsible for such ghastliness.

The guilty ones must be named.

They are none other than 'the authorities'.

They and they alone must take full responsibility for the 'day of infamy'.

And why?

Because basic common sense should have told them that their actions could have done nothing else than provoke unseemly violence, outright mutiny and rowdyism of a type only normally seen at an annual conference of the Conservative and Unionist party.

Putting it quite simply – it was just asking for trouble locking me in the pavilion gents urinals with Mr K. D. 'Slasher' Mackay.

From that and from nothing else stemmed what will forever be known in the annals of our 'summer game' as 'The Troubles'.

As calmly as I can I shall now describe the events of that fateful day.

As always on the Saturday of the Lords Test I arose at three thirty in the morning so as not to disturb the lady wife and her confounded Bedlington terriers and made my way in stockinged feet through the rose shrubberies where friends were waiting for me with 'a fast car'.

How comforting the clink of brandy flask.

How heady the scent of fine malt whisky.

How beautiful the unfolding panorama of our dear English countryside as dawn spread her rosy fingers over pasture and water meadow, over mist-shrouded cattle and sentinel heron, over slumbering thatch and sputtering rill.

We arrived at our club in good time for breakfast.

How comforting the clink of brandy flask.

How heady the scent of malt whisky.

How the gastric juices quickened to the tang of sizzling gammon, plump sausages, butter-drenched mushroom, spitting kidney, snarling steak, tight-coiled chop and purring, golden eggs.

How the palate crooned to the caress of rich and noble claret.

And how comforting the clink of brandy flask and how heady the scent of fine malt whisky.

And then to Lords.

Lords in all its finery.

Lords *en fête*.

Lords ablaze in the glory of distinguished Test

cricketers, both old and young.

What a panopoly of talent.

I spotted at once Lord Harris and Sir Jack Hobbs, and within the hour had seen and spoken to such luminaries as Alec Bedser, Eric Bedser, Alec Bedser, Eric Bedser, and a gloomy fellow in shapeless grey suit and nylon socks who looked remarkably like Alec Bedser and his brother, Eric.

The first hint of trouble came when I found a man of unmistakeable colonial appearance ensconced in my chair in the Brian Close Memorial Bar in the pavilion.

He was dressed in a wide-brimmed hat with one side affixed to the crown, snuff-stained khaki drill jacket, navy blue PT shorts and hiker's boots and seemed to be under the impression that I was called 'Blue'.

Dodging the brown stream of chewing tobacco which squirted from the side of his mouth, I examined the badge on the lapel of his drill jacket and discovered that the brute was none other than Mr Keith Miller's grandmother.

I summoned Griffiths from his office to remove the creature, and in the ensuing fracas received a severe bite on my left buttock and had the clasp of an MCC cufflink buckled beyond redemption.

This was to prove a minor irritation in the light of subsequent events.

After settling myself in my chair (somewhat painfully I am bound to confess) I summoned the head waiter, Bailey, to fetch me a bottle of my usual Brown and Robertson vintage tawny port.

'Sorry, sir,' said the lugubrious, obsequious Bailey, 'We've sold out.'

'Sold out?' I bellowed.

'Yes, sir,' said Bailey. 'Not a bottle left in the place.'

In the ensuing fracas I received superficial flesh wounds on both elbows, and had the point of an MCC tie-pin most painfully embedded two inches to the sou' sou' east of my left nipple.

What could have turned into a most 'ugly scene' was curtailed by an announcement that there would be no play before luncheon.

The cheer which went up in the bar was indicative of the relief felt by one and all that our imbibing activities would not be disturbed by the necessity of having to watch a cricket match which to one and all was an irritating diversion to the main purpose of the event – the reunion of old friends and colleagues, the swapping of yarns and badinage and the celebration of one hundred years of incredibly boring cricket articles written by Mr E. W. 'Gloria' Swanton.

As we looked anxiously at the lowering clouds one question was uppermost in our minds – would the bloody things suddenly lift, dry out the pitch and so completely spoil our day?

It was in the manner shown by generation of Englishmen beleaguered in rotting Flanders trench, steamy African jungle and Tesco cash desk that with stiff upper lips and steely eyes we faced this danger.

I found myself in the company of a dwarf-like figure with large ears name of Hazlitt or Harsnett or Hassett who claimed to have captained his country at Test match level.

To me he looked more like an undertaker suffering from a chronic attack of piles, and I felt bound to appraise him of my views.

In the ensuing fracas I received a stinging blow behind the right temple and was damn near garrotted by Mr Geoffrey Boycott's jock strap.

However, once again fate intervened in the form of another announcement on the public address system to the effect that the museum at the back of the pavilion was shortly to be opened with an exhibition of Mr Gil Langley's underpants.

Chairs were overturned, tables were knocked asunder as eager members fought and scratched with each other to gain a favourable place at the head of the queue outside the museum.

Peace, blessed peace, reigned in the bar.

Once more united with my friends, I established myself at a strategic point near the entrance to the gents urinals and soon we were soothing our tattered nerves with generous supplies of an excellent 1974 Schloss Blofeld Spätauslese.

It was during this blissful lull that I and my friends heard the words which sent shivers of fear and mortification rilling down the length of our respective spines.

In a dark corner of the bar, standing next to the space invader machines, were two figures clad in white coats, one of whom was drinking Vimto out of a large panama hat.

The umpires!

And they were deep in conversation.

We held our breath.

We strained our ears.

And then we heard those terrifying words:

'Right then, Dicky. We'll tell them – we resume play

immediately after lunch.'

In the ensuing fracas I received several sharp kicks in my private parts and was set upon by several burly men who smelled strongly of fresh score cards and Tavener's fruit drops.

Despite my frenzied protestations and struggles I was forcibly thrown into the gents urinals and there as I slid and slithered on the tiled floor I heard the unmistakable sound of a padlock being applied to the outside of the door.

I leapt to my feet.

I hammered at the door.

I heaved at the handle.

I shouted. I bellowed.

All to no avail.

I was locked in.

And then suddenly I was aware of another's presence.

I turned.

And there placidly standing at a stall attending to a 'call of nature' was none other than Mr K. D. 'Slasher' Mackay of Queensland and Australia.

To see him standing there so cool, calm and collected set off a chain of emotions in me, which to this day remain blurred and confused.

Suffice it to say that in the ensuing fracas several articles of a plumbing nature were detached from the walls of the urinal and I was knocked into oblivion by a particularly large Edrich and Compton patent ballcock.

How long I remained unconscious I do not know.

I remember waking slowly to hear on the public address system an announcement that owing to unfortunate and unforeseen circumstances in the pavilion the entire urinal facilities of the ground had been rendered inoperative.

The effect was instantaneous.

Imagine it — twenty to thirty thousand healthy red-blooded English males denied an outlet for one of the most basic and fundamental of human needs.

Thus the outcry.

Thus the uproar.

Thus the assault on umpires.

Thus the abuse of committee members of MCC.

Thus the clamour and the violence.

Thus the fact that despite the appearance of strong sunshine and a brisk drying wind in mid-afternoon, the pitch remained sodden.

Well, there was only one place available for the twenty to thirty thousand healthy, red-blooded English males to. . .

I was there.

Oh yes, I was there.

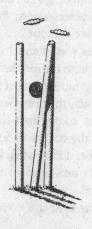

13

Incident at Frome

Our beloved 'summer game' abounds in stories and anecdotes of characters whom we cricket lovers traditionally term 'larger than life'.

Such a character was Himmelweit.

It is my intention to recount his singular history.

And 'singular' is indeed a most pertinent word to use, for Himmelweit was the only German in the history of the 'summer game' to play first-class county cricket.

He played for the county of Somerset from the year 1919 until the year 1921, when he became the central figure in what is now known to historians as 'The incident at Frome'.

Himmelweit came to this country in the year 1916

when his Zeppelin was shot down during a bombing raid on Shepton Mallet – thus giving him residential qualifications to play for Somerset.

He was deposited forthwith into prison – thus giving him residential qualifications to play for Wormwood Scrubs.

He first came to the notice of the cricketing authorities when he appeared in the match, Minor Counties versus Huns, at Much Wenlock.

Minor Counties were skippered by Jas Humberstone senior.

Huns were skippered by Thomas Mann, a minor literary figure, who was later to achieve wider fame as the father and grandfather respectively of F. G. and F. T. Mann of Middlesex and England.

Minor Counties won the toss and elected to bat.

The innings was opened by Jas Humberstone, Senior, and the former Leicestershire professional, Amiss, later to achieve wider fame as the father and grandfather respectively of the two cricketing brothers, Dennis and Kingsley.

The Huns skipper tossed the crimson rambler to Himmelweit to open the bowling.

Humberstone crouched at the crease in his typical aggressive stance, and as he faced to the bowling the buckles of his braces flashed angrily, the ferrets in his hip pocket gnashed their teeth and the clank of steel dentures echoed round the ground.

'Right, Fritz,' he growled. 'Do your worst.'

It was to be one of the most memorable moments in the history of the 'summer game'.

Himmelweit commenced his run.

One stride, two strides, three strides.

It was indeed a fearsome sight as his iron crosses clattered and his cavalry sabre splintered the weak Shropshire sunlight into myriads of sparkling fragments.

Nearer and nearer he approached the wicket, and as he did so spectators became aware of a curious whistling sound.

Louder and louder it grew.

Ghastly.

Horrendous.

A banshee howl that caused spectators to clasp their ears in agony, for all the world like the unsuspecting audience at a Cliff Richard concert.

And then Himmelweit reached the wicket and delivered the ball. It was a masterly delivery; full length, pitched on middle and leg and veering sharply to off with a snakelike whiplash.

Humberstone's castle was wrecked.

That well-known cricket writer, Mr Neville Cardew, later to achieve even wider fame as the father and grandfather respectively of the distinguished wit and raconteur, Mr Cardew Robinson, wrote in his journal the following:

'I doubt whether any man alive – or dead – could have played that ball.

'Even though Humberstone at the moment of delivery was stretched on the ground writhing in contortions of agony, hands clamped tight to his auditory orifices, I am of the firm opinion that the perfect pitch and pace of the ball would have beaten his forward defensive prod and caused him forthwith to give no trouble to the scorer.'

Thus did the carnage begin.

The Minor Counties were dismissed for five, Himmelweit taking all ten wickets at a cost of only one run, this being solely due to a piece of grossly negligent ground fielding by the young Otto Klemperer.

The Huns in the person of their two openers, the Umlaut brothers, A. P. F. and J. W. H. N. S. – the latter known affectionately as Johnny Will Heute Nicht Schlagen – knocked off the runs required in one over thus winning the match by ten wickets.

The Minor Counties players were incensed, but it was some time later during the subsequent fracas in the tea tent that the source of the whistling sound, which had caused them so much distress, was discovered.

Himmelweit, with typical Teutonic baseness of behaviour, had affixed to the inside of his kneecap a device used by the German gunners in their howitzers during the bombardment of Beauvais to strike terror into the hearts of the Allied horses.

This prompted Humberstone, senior's, celebrated remark:

'It might not have done much for the horses, but, by God, it frightened the living shits out of me.'

Dear Jas Humberstone. But for the vileness of his tongue and his total lack of Christian charity he would have made a spendid archbishop of Canterbury – he had exactly the right size of shifty, untrustworthy eyes.

To return to Much Wenlock; the shock waves of this incident reverberated throughout the land.

Questions were asked in Parliament. A meeting of the Privy Council was summoned. All the regiments of the Scottish Highland Division were put on immediate alert, and Mrs Mary Whitehouse wrote a letter of protest to Mr Billy Cotton, junior, father and grandfather of the celebrated golfer, Joseph, and the distinguished moving kinematograph star, Henry.

As a result of all this activity there was formulated what is now known to historians of the 'summer game' as the Much Wenlock Amendment.

I quote:

'The implements of the game.

'Note Seven B.

'Articles of ordnance or artillery may not normally be used during the course of the match except by the prior agreement of the two captains, who must notify forthwith the umpires, if the said articles contain matter of an explosive nature which may cause distress or injury to domestic animals and agricultural livestock in the immediate vicinity of the ground.'

Despite the various unpleasantnesses which resulted from this match, Himmelweit's services were eagerly sought by all the first-class counties with the exception of Yorkshire, of course, who still to this day refuse to allow players of German birth or independent nature to play for the county.

It was left to MCC to decide that the enforced landing of Himmelweit's Zeppelin on Somerset soil gave that county the right to claim his services.

This rule is still in operation with a suitable amendment to deal with the accidental landing of flying saucers and the alien beings contained therein.

(It is believed that Northamptonshire have benefited most in recent times from this amendment.)

Himmelweit's deeds with Somerset require little embellishment from me.

The records speak for themselves.

Let us dwell for a moment on matters of a more personal nature.

I myself met Himmelweit personally on numerous occasions, and I can say without fear or flattery that of all the county cricketers of his era he was without doubt the most offensive and nauseating man it has ever been my misfortune to encounter.

The stiff bow of the head when he was introduced, the clicking of heels and the guttural growlings from the back of the throat seemed totally inappropriate from a first-class county cricketer – although some years later, I am bound to confess, it was made acceptable by the behaviour of Mr E. R. Dexter on entering the television commentary box at 'headquarters'.

There were times, also, when it seemed Himmelweit went out of his way to antagonize both team mate and opponent alike.

While the majority of players were content during drinks intervals to accept orange or grapefruit crush, Himmelweit insisted on a half bottle of lightly chilled Bernkasteler Niersteiner Domtal.

And on finishing this he would invariably hurl his glass to the ground and grind it underfoot with his spurs – an act which was subsequently found to be the cause of the untimely demise of the groundsman's horse at Cheltenham.

While most players, too, were content to take a light salad during the luncheon adjournment, Himmelweit insisted on a full five-course meal consisting of Bauernschmeiss mit Knackwurst, Sauerkraut mit Bratkartoffeln, Bayerische Obsttorte, Kaffee mit Schlag and Kirschknoedel à la mode Harry Makepeace.

Himmelweit fell foul of umpires, too, by insisting on appealing in his native tongue.

'Wie ist das?' he would shout in a blood-curdling yell.

And when he came to the wicket to take guard, he would scowl at the umpire and growl:

'Mittel und Bein.'

Many years later when talking about this the celebrated umpire, Mr George Pope, who was later to achieve wider fame as the father and grandfather respectively of the two Popes, John Paul 1 and John Paul 11, was heard to remark:

'Ah'd 'ave let t'booger rot, if he'd not 'ad decency to say *bitte schön.*'

I am indebted for this anecdote to the delightful memoirs of that most subtle of cricket writers, Mr Alan Gibson, father of Althea Gibson, the first black player ever to win a Wimbledon championship.

Himmelweit was never popular in his adopted county.

Somerset is an essentially rural county and many people in the Taunton area were convinced that it was Himmelweit with his Teutonic ways who was responsible in the winter of 1920 for a particularly severe outbreak of swine fever.

Certainly it was these suspicions which accounted for his singular lack of support from county members at the time of the infamous 'Incident at Frome'.

I now propose to recount in some detail the circumstances surrounding this occurrence.

It took place during the match against Lancashire who at that time if memory serves me correct (and it usually doesn't) were in strong contention for the county championship.

The Red Rose county had a team of all the talents, including that nonpareil of fast bowlers, the Australian, Mr E. A. McDonald, who was later to achieve even wider fame in the moving kinematograph as the partner of Mr Nelson Eddy.

McDonald was a bowler of awesome speed, a man in the prime of his talents and feared and respected the length and breadth of the country.

The match promised to be a 'humdinger'.

Somerset won the toss, and skipper, Bertie Furze, deliberated long and hard before deciding to bat on a green and lively wicket, expecting, no doubt, Himmelweit to take his toll later in the game.

It was a disastrous decision.

McDonald, bowling at fearsome speed, had the ball rearing and spitting from the very first moment of the game.

Within the space of five overs he had claimed six Somerset wickets and dispatched three of his opponents to hospital suffering from shock, head wounds and indecent exposure.

It was at this moment that Himmelweit appeared at the wicket wearing garb of the most singular appearance.

The Lancashire skipper objected immediately.

The rule book was consulted, but on finding that there was no reference to the wearing of cavalry breast plates, spiked helmets and spurs, play was allowed to continue.

The first ball McDonald bowled to Himmelweit whistled down to a good length and reared like a mortar shell head high.

Himmelweit did not flinch. Instead of ducking he soared into the air and with a movement of the head muscles that would not have disgraced the immortal 'Dixie' Dean, later to achieve even wider fame as the sister of the celebrated light comedienne and chanteuse, Miss Phyllis Dixie, headed the ball first bounce to the boundary.

Incensed, McDonald hurled down a ball of even greater speed.

Once more Himmelweit rose in the air and headed the ball to the boundary.

A six!

McDonald ground his teeth and next ball bowled a vicious delivery that hurtled at Himmelweit's midriff and struck him a sickening blow in the vitals.

Himmelweit stood his ground.

His upper lip curled icily.

The sunlight flashed on his monocle.

And then in a sudden movement he made a crucial adjustment to his dress by covering his vitals with his cavalryman's spiked helmet.

McDonald scowled and bowled again.

Another ferocious ball hurled straight at the most tender of anatomical parts known to man – and sometimes to women.

Clang!

The noise echoed and reverberated the length and breadth of the green and rolling hills of Somerset.

Rooks flew up in alarm, rabbits scurried to their burrows, hens stopped laying, but Himmelweit did not budge.

Defiant and upright he stood.

But where was the ball?

It was the great Dick Tyldesley who spotted it.

It was impaled on the end of the spike on the cavalryman's helmet.

'How's that?' he yelled.

Scarcely had the words left his lips than Himmelweit commenced his run.

'Lauf!' he shouted to his bemused partner, the young Goblet. 'Lauf, englischer Schweinhund!'

For some time the Lancashire players stood in a motionless daze as Himmelweit and his partner commenced to run between the wickets, the ball still attached to the spike on the German's helmet.

Twenty-seven they ran before the immortal Cec Parkin shouted:

'Right, lads. Let's scrag the German sod.'

The subsequent fracas was ghastly to behold.

Lancashire players piled themselves on top of Himmelweit who in cold fury struck out with his sabre.

The gore flowed copiously, and it was not until the arrival of a detachment of the Somerset Light Yeomanry and representatives of the Frome Temperance Fire Brigade that the players were separated.

There was a moment's silence.

And then the immortal Cec Parkin pounced once more.

Pointing at the wicket he shouted:

'How's that?'

Miraculously despite all the violence and the ill feeling the wicket had remained intact – except for the off bail which lay at the side of the popping crease with, entwined around it, an iron cross.

'Out,' said the umpire.

And that to my knowledge is first and only time the dismissal has been written in the scorebook:

'Out. Iron Cross hit wicket.'

But what of Himmelweit?

Of him there was no sign.

Indeed he was never seen again.

Rumour has it that he was taken under armed escort by the Somerset Light Yeomanry to London in the dead of night and there executed by firing squad on the real tennis courts at Lords.

But who can say?

One thing, however, still puzzles me about Himmelweit.

No one ever knew his Christian name.

But then, I don't suppose he was the sort of man to have one.